THE BOBBSEY TWINS:
THE SECRET AT THE SEASHORE

A summer at the seashore with Cousin Dorothy is an exciting enough prospect for the Bobbsey Twins, who, of course, don't know of the other adventures awaiting them there.

Visiting the Lakeside Amusement Park, Bert and Nan, Flossie and Freddie, and Dorothy make a new friend, Cindy, whose father has been lost in an airplane crash at sea. And sharp-eyed Freddie catches a glimpse of the thief who has eluded police after stealing a sackful of $100 bills.

Together the children enjoy all the pleasures of the seashore, but strange and intriguing things keep happening too. Nan finds a bottle washed ashore by the waves, containing a message from someone marooned on an island. And there is the mystery of the vanishing boats. First, the canoe is stolen from the water carnival, then Freddie's toy sailboat floats away to sea, and finally the motorboat vanishes from its mooring.

But the Bobbsey Twins, who love mysteries, eventually put all the clues together to find the answer and win a surprising reward!

THE BOBBSEY TWINS
By Laura Lee Hope

"He's in trouble!" Bert shouted and started to run

The Bobbsey Twins: The Secret at the Seashore

By

LAURA LEE HOPE

GROSSET & DUNLAP

A NATIONAL GENERAL COMPANY

Publishers   *New York*

ISBN: 0–448–08003–6
© GROSSET & DUNLAP, INC., 1962
ALL RIGHTS RESERVED

PRINTED IN THE UNITED STATES OF AMERICA

The Bobbsey Twins: The Secret at the Seashore

CONTENTS

THE BOBBSEY TWINS:
THE SECRET AT THE SEASHORE

CHAPTER I

A WHIRLYBIRD RIDE

"WHAT'S in the box, Freddie?" Bert Bobbsey asked curiously, as the shopping trip ended.

Six-year-old Freddie grinned and shook his blond head. "I can't tell. It's a secret until we get to Ocean Cliff," he replied, his blue eyes sparkling with mischief.

At this moment the rest of the Bobbsey family came from a nearby shop. Tall, athletic Mr. Bobbsey and his pretty wife followed the two girls. Dark-haired, twelve-year-old Nan was Bert's twin.

Flossie, who was Freddie's chubby, blond twin, ran ahead. "Mother bought the prettiest lemonade glasses to take to Aunt Emily!" she cried.

"I have a present for Cousin Dorothy," Freddie announced, "but it's a secret!"

"I have a secret, too!" Mr. Bobbsey said with a chuckle.

1

"Oh, how 'citing!" Flossie clapped her hands and gave a little skip. "Two secrets! What's yours, Daddy?"

"You'll know tomorrow, my little fat fairy!" her father said teasingly. This was his special nickname for his small daughter. He called Freddie his little fireman because Freddie loved to play with toy fire engines.

The Lakeport Bobbseys were visiting Uncle Daniel and Aunt Sarah Bobbsey at their farm on the outskirts of the town of Meadowbrook. They planned to leave in a few days for Ocean Cliff, where they would stay with Mrs. Bobbsey's sister, Aunt Emily Minturn.

The Minturns' daughter Dorothy was the same age as Bert and Nan. She was lively and full of fun, and liked to play jokes.

"I wish tomorrow was here now," Flossie sighed. Then she turned to her twin. "Please, Freddie," she urged, "tell me your secret."

But Freddie only smiled and clutched the small brown cardboard box more closely.

"I'll be sorry to leave Meadowbrook," Nan remarked as they drove toward the farm, "but it will be fun to see Dorothy again."

"And to swim in the ocean," Bert added. "I'm going to work on my crawl while we're there."

"I'll bet I can swim 'most all the way across the ocean!" Freddie boasted.

Flossie giggled. "It's too far. You wouldn't get back in time for supper!"

"Well, maybe I won't go all the way," Freddie decided.

After Mr. Bobbsey had parked the car near the farmhouse, Freddie jumped out and ran into the kitchen.

"Will you help me with my surprise, Dinah?" he asked a jolly-looking colored woman who was lifting a pan of biscuits from the oven.

Dinah Johnson had helped Mrs. Bobbsey with the housework as long as the children could remember. She often went with them when they visited their relatives. Dinah's husband Sam drove a truck at Mr. Bobbsey's lumberyard in Lakeport, and the couple lived in an apartment on the third floor of the Bobbsey home.

"What you got there?" Dinah asked suspiciously as she put the pan on a table.

Freddie stood on tiptoes and whispered in her ear. A broad smile broke over Dinah's kindly face.

"You just leave it to me," she said with a chuckle as she took the cardboard box. "I'll take good care of this surprise until we go to Ocean Cliff."

"Thanks, Dinah," the little boy said gratefully and ran out of the kitchen.

Later, the twins' cousin, Harry Bobbsey, remarked wistfully, "I wish I was going to Ocean Cliff with you. Something exciting always happens wherever you go!"

"I wish you could come, too," Bert agreed. "I'd like to have another boy to fool around with."

"But you'll be busy taking care of Major, Harry," Nan spoke up.

Major was Harry's prize bull. In the BOBBSEY TWINS' ADVENTURE IN THE COUNTRY, Major had been stolen, and it was only after good detective work by the twins that he had been found again and the thieves caught.

"When will we know your secret, Daddy?" Flossie asked, a moment later.

"I expect a phone call tomorrow morning," Mr. Bobbsey replied. "After that I should be able to tell you about it."

It seemed a long time before the telephone rang the next morning. When Mr. Bobbsey came back to the breakfast table after taking the call, four eager faces were turned in his direction.

"Come on, Dad, tell us what it is," Bert pleaded as his father seated himself and began to eat again.

"Oh, that call?" Mr. Bobbsey said teasingly, putting down his fork. "Well, it's this. How would you all like to go to Ocean Cliff in a whirlybird?"

"Whirlybird? What kind of bird is that?" Flossie asked in bewilderment.

Her father laughed. "A helicopter."

"Oh, I know," said Flossie. "It's like an airplane. Only it has whirling things on top so it can fly straight up and down."

"Say, Dad," cried Bert, "that would be great!"

"A whirlybird!" Freddie shouted. "We're going in a whirlybird!"

"Will there be room for us all?" Mrs. Bobbsey inquired.

The twins' father explained that the telephone call had been from a business friend of his, whose firm owned the helicopter. "Mr. Nixon suggested we might enjoy the trip. The copter has seats for fifteen, but he thinks we'd better not count on taking more than six passengers since the helicopter will have to carry extra fuel for such a distance."

Dinah had come in to clear the breakfast table. "That's just fine," she said with a big smile. "Old Dinah doesn't like flying through the air. Snoop and I—we'll go on the train!"

"I don't think Downy would like to fly so high either," Freddie said anxiously.

Snoop was the Bobbseys' black cat, and

Downy was a pet duck which Harry had given his little cousin.

"That's settled then," Mr. Bobbsey remarked. "You twins and your mother and I will go in the copter and take the luggage. Dinah can take the animals on the train. Mr. Nixon says his pilot will land on the front lawn here tomorrow morning at nine o'clock."

"Daddy, you think of the most 'citingest things!" Flossie exclaimed, jumping up and running over to hug her father.

The children were busy the rest of the day gathering together their belongings for Mrs. Bobbsey and Dinah to pack. Then with Harry they made a farewell tour of the farm, saying good-by to all the animals.

"We've had such a wonderful time!" Nan said.

"I hope you'll all come again next summer," Harry said. "Maybe there'll be another mystery to solve."

The next morning Uncle Daniel took Dinah to town to catch the early train. She had Snoop and Downy, the duck, in two wicker carrying baskets.

Promptly at nine o'clock there was a loud whirring sound overhead. Both Bobbsey families dashed to the front lawn in time to see a banana-shaped craft settle down on the grass. It had two whirling rotors, one in front over the glass-enclosed pilot's compartment, and another over the up-slanting tail.

"Look!" Bert pointed. "It has pontoons so it can land on water!"

A smiling young man with curly black hair

came down the steps which were attached to the door, and lowered them when it was opened.

"Good morning!" he called cheerfully. "I'm Don Wheaton. All set for Ocean Cliff?"

Mr. Bobbsey shook hands, then introduced the pilot to the others.

"We'll put your luggage in here," the young man said, opening a door in the tail of the heli-copter.

"I'll take my box inside with me," Freddie explained. "It's a surprise for my cousin Dorothy."

After many good-bys the Lakeport Bobbseys climbed into the aircraft. Double seats ranged along one side with a narrow aisle between them and the windows on the other side.

"Lots of room, folks," Don Wheaton pointed out. "Sit anywhere you like."

Mr. and Mrs. Bobbsey chose seats toward the front while Bert and Nan settled themselves near the middle.

"Let's sit in back, Freddie," Flossie proposed, sliding into the rear pair of seats.

When all the passengers were settled, the pilot locked the door and went forward to his compartment. In another moment the roar of the rotors filled the cabin, the craft gave a shiver, then began to rise slowly from the lawn.

The children waved from the windows as the mechanical bird rose vertically from the farm. Finally the helicopter began to move forward and the twins leaned back in their seats.

"It's noisy, isn't it?" Bert shouted to Nan.

She nodded, intent on picking out familiar landmarks as they passed beneath the aircraft.

In the rear seats Flossie leaned toward her twin. "Please show me your surprise for Dorothy," she pleaded. "I won't tell anyone else."

With a grin Freddie opened one end of the

cardboard box, which had holes punched in the top. Flossie peered in.

"Ooh, how cute!" she cried. "What is it?"

"He's a hamster and his name is Twinkle," Freddie explained. "He's sort of like a tiny rabbit or squirrel."

"I want to hold him." Flossie put her hand into the box and drew out the little reddish-brown animal. She held the soft, furry pet up to her cheek.

Just at that moment the helicopter hit an air pocket and dropped slightly. Without thinking, Flossie opened her hand. The hamster fell to the floor. The next instant it went scurrying up the aisle.

"Get him!" Freddie yelled over the noise of the helicopter. "Catch Twinkle!"

Bert and Nan saw the tiny animal scampering past and jumped to their feet. The hamster disappeared through the open doorway into the pilot's compartment. Bert and Nan were in close pursuit.

Bert caught sight of Freddie's pet cowering in a corner. Dropping to his knees, the boy crept forward, then gently closed his hand over the trembling little creature.

"If this is your surprise for Dorothy," Bert said with a grin as he handed the hamster to Freddie, "you'd better hang on to it."

"Thanks, Bert," said Freddie. "I'd better put Twinkle back in his box."

Nan was excited by the view from the pilot's compartment. The nose of the helicopter was like a large glass bubble which gave a complete picture in all directions.

Seeing her interest, the pilot motioned to the empty seat beside him. "Stay up here for a while if you like," he suggested. "I'm glad to have company."

Nan sat down. Don Wheaton pointed out various sights below them. Then suddenly the whir of the propellers became louder and the whirlybird lurched to one side.

"Oh, oh," Don muttered, "we're in for a little blow." A faraway look came into his eyes. "Wind storms always make me feel sad," he said. "A pilot friend of mine, Pete Weller, was lost in one. Nobody has heard from him in months."

"How dreadful!" said Nan.

The wind grew stronger as they neared Ocean Cliff. Finally Don Wheaton said to Nan, "You'd better get back to your regular place now, and tell everyone to fasten his seat belt."

By the time Nan reached Bert's side the copter was bouncing and twisting in the gusts of wind. One minute it seemed to stand still, then with a shudder it would go on. From the windows the Bobbseys could see that they were flying along the coast.

"We must be almost to Ocean Cliff. We won't have much more of this," Mr. Bobbsey said reassuringly.

"But, Dad," Nan said worriedly, "will we be able to land in this wind?"

CHAPTER II

THE LIFEGUARD'S SURPRISE

NAN waited tensely for her father's reply. He shook his head uncertainly.

"Dad," said Bert, nodding toward the front of the helicopter where the pilot had turned in his seat. "I think Don wants to speak to you."

Mr. Bobbsey unfastened his seat belt and struggled forward. At the doorway of the pilot's compartment he held a brief conversation with the pilot.

When he came back he motioned Freddie, Flossie, Bert, and Nan to come to the front of the whirlybird and take seats.

"Don thinks he may have to land on the water," Mr. Bobbsey explained. "In that case he wants us to put on life vests. They're under the seats."

Quickly the twins pulled the vests from their containers. The helicopter was pitching so violently that they could not stand, so they turned in their seats and helped one another adjust the jackets.

"Won't Dorothy be surprised to see us swimming ashore?" Nan said, trying to sound cheerful.

The small twins giggled. Then all the Bobbseys became quiet as they listened to the roar of the rotors fighting to keep the craft aloft.

Suddenly Bert shouted, "We're coming down on the beach! Look! There are Aunt Emily and Uncle William and Dorothy!"

The helicopter settled down on the wide strip of smooth sand. The next moment the rotors stopped and Don came back to the cabin with a relieved smile on his ruddy face.

"Well, we made it, folks!" he said. "And no-one got his feet wet!"

"It was a swell ride," Bert exclaimed.

The door was opened, and the Bobbseys hurried down the steps into the welcoming arms of the Minturns. When all the greetings were over, Mr. Bobbsey, Mr. Minturn, Bert, and Don began to take the luggage from the tail of the helicopter.

Freddie held out the brown cardboard box to slender, dark-eyed Dorothy. "I brought you a surprise present," he said. "His name is Twinkle."

Dorothy opened the end of the box and peered in. "Oh, Freddie!" she exclaimed. "It's a hamster! I've always wanted one. Thanks a million!"

"When we get to the house, I'll tell you how to take care of him," Freddie told her.

Don Wheaton said he must get back to his company's airfield. After many thanks from the Bobbseys, the curly-haired pilot climbed into the helicopter. The rotors spun, and in another few minutes the sausage-like craft was whirring off into the distance.

"Nan, you and Flossie are going to stay in my room with me," Dorothy chattered as the group made their way up to the Minturns' house on the cliff. "There's loads of space, and I thought it would be more fun that way."

"That's great!" Nan replied with a laugh. "We can talk all night!"

When the children reached the house, Dorothy said, "I have a surprise for you. Follow me."

She led them around the house to the old barn and flung open the door. "There they are!" Inside were two small gray burros!

"Oh, aren't they darling!" Nan exclaimed. Flossie ran up to pat the little animals.

"Their names are Doodle and Dandy," Dorothy told her cousins. "I have a cart, too. We'll take a ride some day soon."

"Oh, yes," Flossie cried. "Maybe Freddie and I can drive."

As they neared the house again, Uncle William was just about to leave for the station to meet Dinah. Freddie asked to go along. "I can't wait to see Snoop and Downy," he explained.

After the train pulled in and Dinah got off, she reported that both the cat and the duck seemed to have enjoyed their trip.

"Why don't you put Downy on the little pond at the side of the house, Freddie?" Uncle William suggested when they reached his house again.

Freddie carefully carried Downy to the pond and set him on the quiet water. The duck paddled off happily. Dorothy brought a cage from the attic for the hamster, and he settled down contentedly. The children ate lunch, then went outside.

"Let's see how Downy likes the pond," Flossie proposed. The others ran with her to the pond.

Suddenly Freddie stopped at the edge of the water. "Why, where is he?" the little boy asked in bewilderment. "Downy's gone!"

"Here comes somebody who may know where he is—Hal Bingham," said Dorothy.

She introduced the twins to a tall boy who seemed to be slightly older than Bert. He had a merry twinkle in his dark eyes.

"What's this? You've lost a duck?" he asked.

After Freddie had told him all about Downy, Hal turned to Dorothy. "You know the water from this pond runs down that little waterfall under the road into the ocean."

"Waterfall!" Freddie cried. "Do you think Downy has gone over the falls?" He dashed around the house and down the path to the beach. The others ran after him.

"I see him! I see him!" Freddie called, pointing out over the ocean. There was the little duck bobbing up and down far out on the waves.

Quick as a flash Flossie raced along the beach toward the lifeguard's tower. A tanned young man was seated on the sand in front of it.

"Come quick!" Flossie cried. "Downy's in the ocean and he's drowning!"

"Okay, I'll get him," the lifeguard called back, running toward a rowboat at the edge of the water. In another minute he was pulling with strong strokes in the direction Flossie had pointed.

At the sight of the running lifeguard, the other people on the beach stood up, straining their eyes to watch the rescue.

"Wait until they find out he's gone after a duck!" Hal remarked to Bert with a chuckle.

By this time the young lifeguard had reached the bobbing yellow speck on the waves. The

Flossie raced along the beach toward the lifeguard's tower

children saw him stop rowing and lean over the side of the boat.

"He has Downy!" Flossie cried happily.

A few minutes later the lifeguard beached his boat and carried the duck up to the waiting children. A wave of laughter swept over the onlookers.

"Thank you for rescuing him," Freddie said solemnly as he cradled Downy in his arms.

"Flossie didn't mean to make you think a person was out there drowning," Bert apologized. "She was just upset about the duck."

The young man laughed. "That's all right, son," he said. "We don't stop to ask questions when we think anyone's in trouble. I'm glad I could save your pet."

"Where can we keep Downy now?" Freddie wailed. "He'll swim away again."

"I'll fix that for you," Hal spoke up. "We have some wire netting in our boathouse. I'll fasten a piece of it along the top of the falls. Then Downy can't swim out of the pond."

Bert went with his new friend, and in a short time they had blocked the pond.

"Let's go swimming," Dorothy suggested when the boys had finished.

Everyone thought this was a good idea, and soon the six children gathered on the beach in their suits.

"How would you and Freddie like to have a chicken fight?" Hal asked Flossie, when the small twins had grown tired of playing at the edge of the water.

"I'd rather have a duck fight," Freddie objected.

Hal laughed. "Okay, we'll make it ducks."

He explained the game. Then he lifted Freddie onto his shoulders while Bert did the same with Flossie. The boys walked out into the ocean until the water was at their shoulders. Then they turned to face each other.

"Now, ducks, start fighting!" Hal cried. At the signal, Freddie and Flossie began splashing each other with water.

Hal and Bert jumped around to make it harder for each twin to reach the other. Flossie laughed so hard and flailed the water so fast that she lost her balance and tumbled from Bert's shoulders.

He had a firm hold on her legs so she only got a ducking. "I like duck fighting," she spluttered as Bert set her on his shoulders again.

"I won! I won!" Freddie shouted. "Flossie fell off!"

"I'll beat you the next time," Flossie insisted as the older boys waded to shore with their "ducks."

"I think Nan and I should be the ducks tomorrow," Dorothy remarked. "How about it, Hal?"

"Sure," he agreed. "I'll meet you all on the beach tomorrow morning."

"So long," Bert called as the tall boy left. "I'm glad you're here to keep all the girls from picking on me."

"Is that so!" said Dorothy. "You haven't seen anything yet!"

During the night the wind came up again, and by morning the ocean was a mass of whitecaps.

"I'm afraid it's too rough for you children to go swimming today," Aunt Emily observed in the living room after breakfast. Then, seeing their disappointed looks, she continued, "Perhaps we could go to Lakeside Amusement Park."

Mrs. Minturn explained that a new amusement park had been opened along the shore of a large lake which was a short distance back of Ocean Cliff. Most of the residents of the cliff kept their boats moored on the lake.

"Our outboard motorboat is there, too," Dorothy explained. "We call it the *Firefly*."

"What a pretty name!" said Nan.

Flossie was more interested in seeing the amusement park. "Let's go right away!" she urged.

Dorothy ran to phone Hal and tell him the change in plans. She came back saying, "Hal is going into the city with his father, so he won't be able to come with us."

"That's too bad," Bert remarked. "Well, it means you kids will have to take orders from just Freddie and me." He dashed away before Dorothy could throw a pillow at him.

Mr. Bobbsey asked to be excused from the trip. "William and I have plans to go fishing."

The children quickly got ready for the trip to the amusement park. When they reached it, Mrs. Minturn stopped to buy tickets at the big entrance gate. The group walked across a bridge and into the main part of the park.

Then they stopped in surprise. There were policemen everywhere!

CHAPTER III

UNDERGROUND CITY

"WHAT do you suppose has happened?" Bert asked in astonishment.

"Perhaps we should leave and come another time," Mrs. Bobbsey suggested.

"Oh, Mother, it must be all right or they wouldn't have let us in," Nan ventured.

Her mother smiled. She knew her children loved mysteries and would never want to leave any place where something mysterious had happened.

"Let's find out what's the matter," Bert said, and they walked up to a policeman who was standing nearby.

In reply to the boy's question, the officer said that a man suspected of stealing a large sum of money had been traced to Lakeside.

"It's like looking for a needle in a haystack," the policeman declared with a discouraged shake of his head. "There are too many places in this park for a person to hide!"

"Who is the man?" Nan asked curiously. "And where was the money stolen from?"

"He worked for Allied Cargo Airlines down the road. They brought in a big shipment of cash from Switzerland this morning and, during the unloading, a lot of it disappeared."

"And they think this man took the money?" Bert questioned.

"That's right," the officer answered. "He was helping to unload the plane, and by the time the loss was discovered he had vanished. Fellow at the airport gate saw him heading this way. We have all the entrances and exits covered."

"Boy," said Bert. "You have quite a puzzle on your hands!"

"What does the man look like?" Freddie asked.

The policeman smiled. "Well, my boy," he said, "they tell me he is short and slim and has yellow hair like yours. Only his hair sticks up on top in a cowlick. That's the description on Albert Garry's record card at the airport."

"We're the Bobbseys," Bert said. He introduced his mother and brother and sisters and then Aunt Emily and Dorothy.

"Pleased to meet you all." The officer took off his cap. "I'm Joe Weaver."

"Maybe we can help you, Officer Weaver," Bert said. "We Bobbseys have helped solve a few mysteries. We might be able to find Albert Garry."

"If you see anyone who fits his description, call headquarters or let me know," Officer Weaver requested.

Promising that they would do this, the Bobbseys and Minturns walked on into the amusement park.

"I hope we can find that man who stole the money," Flossie said earnestly as she skipped along beside Freddie.

"Maybe he's hiding on one of the rides," her twin suggested.

Bert overheard him. "That's a thought," he declared. "Let's separate and look for Garry."

"Okay," said Nan. She saw a roller coaster ahead. "Dorothy, you and Flossie and I can go on that."

Freddie, pointing to a ticket booth not far away, asked, "Will you go in the Underground City with me, Bert?"

"It's fun," Dorothy put in. "You get in little boats which are pulled by a cable through an underground canal. Along the sides are scenes of a make-believe city."

"Where will Mother and Aunt Emily go?" Flossie asked.

Mrs. Bobbsey laughed. "We'll sit here on one of these benches and watch for the thief."

"Hold him until we get back!" Freddie advised as he followed Bert toward the Underground City entrance.

Nan bought tickets for the roller coaster. In another minute she and Dorothy had taken seats in one of the little cars, while Flossie settled between them. A stout woman and a small man in a felt fishing hat sat behind the children.

"I'm going to put on my scarf," Nan announced, pulling a square of bright red silk from her pocket. As she tied it under her chin the car gave a jerk and started up the long incline.

The car reached the top and hurtled down the steep grade ahead. Then it raced up the next piece of track.

"Whee!" Flossie squealed.

"Look at the lake!" Dorothy cried. It seemed as if the speeding car was about to shoot out over the water.

The stout woman clutched the back of the girls' seat. "Let me out, Albert!" she screamed. "This car's going too fast!"

Albert! Could this be the thief Albert Garry? The girls did not dare turn around yet to get a better look at him.

"Now, Minnie," the man said soothingly,

"you know you like roller coasters. The ride will be over in a few minutes!"

The speeding car jerked around a curve. "My hat!" the man yelled as it sailed off into the air.

The next moment Nan gasped, "My scarf!" The wind had caught the fluttering silk and snatched it from her head. Down, down it drifted toward the ground.

A few minutes later the car reached the end of the ride and slowed to a stop. At once the girls turned to look at "Albert." He was completely bald!

"He's not the thief Albert," Dorothy whispered. "Anyway, I don't think a person could hide on the roller coaster!"

Flossie, relieved, said, "That ride was fun!"

"It sure was!" Dorothy agreed. "But my stomach's all mixed up!"

"Maybe we can find your scarf, Nan," Flossie said hopefully.

"Let's look," her sister replied.

The three girls walked slowly around the base of the roller coaster, peering at the ground. When they had reached the ticket booth again Nan looked up. She began to laugh. "Look!" she cried. "On the merry-go-round!"

The revolving platform was halted at the moment. Draped over the head of the tallest giraffe was Nan's red scarf!

"Ooh, doesn't he look funny?" Flossie giggled.

"Come on, let's take a ride," Dorothy urged. "I'll get the scarf for you!"

When the merry-go-round started up again, Dorothy was astride the giraffe. As the music began to play, she grabbed the scarf and

stretched forward to hand it to Nan, who was seated on a tiger in front of her.

"Thanks," Nan said, then chuckled. "I wonder if the bald man got back his hat!"

In the meantime Bert and Freddie had climbed into the little two-passenger boat for the trip through the Underground City. Bert sat in the front seat, with Freddie directly behind him.

"Keep your hands inside the boat!" the attendant called as the boys began to move away.

The first few minutes of the ride were in darkness. Then a lighted scene appeared to one side of the boat. There was a toy service station with several cars. One was having gasoline put into its tank, while a tire was being changed on another. This work was being done by two little moving toy figures.

"Stop the boat!" Freddie urged. "I want to see them longer!"

Bert laughed. "Can't do that. Look, here comes another scene."

This time, the action was on the other side. There was a miniature school building. Children were moving in and out of the front entrance. In the playground was a tiny seesaw with two little figures bobbing up and down. At one side two boys were tossing a ball into a basket fastened to a pole about a foot high.

The boat glided past several more scenes. One was a busy street with little cars obeying the red and green traffic signals. Another was a drive-in movie with a tiny screen flickering in front of a group of toy automobiles.

"Wow! Look at this next one, Freddie!" Bert called.

The little boat had turned a corner. The scene was the largest yet. It showed a block of toy buildings. The one at the far end, labeled Hotel, was afire!

"Oh boy! Look at the fire engine!" Freddie cried in excitement.

The toy engine was standing in front of the building. Little figures of firemen played a stream of water from a long hose on the burning structure.

"The firemen are rescuing the people!" Freddie exclaimed. He pointed to the side of the building where a tiny ladder stretched to the top windows. Firemen were swarming up it.

Suddenly Freddie leaned forward and grabbed Bert's arm. "Look!" he whispered. "There's a man's head behind that middle building!"

"I don't see anything. You're kidding!" Bert protested.

"No, I'm not. He had blond hair and it stuck up on top!" Freddie insisted.

"You must be mistaken, Freddie," Bert said patiently. "I don't think anyone could get in behind there."

Freddie said nothing more. The little boat glided past a park with tiny trees and sparkling ponds. Then it went through a long, dark stretch and finally emerged into the sunlight again.

Mrs. Bobbsey, Aunt Emily, and the three girls were waiting on the platform. "Where's Freddie?" Flossie called out.

"Why, he's—" Bert turned around.

The back seat was empty!

CHAPTER IV

THE FAIRY CASTLE

"BERT!" Mrs. Bobbsey cried in alarm. "Has anything happened to Freddie?"

Her older son was too stunned to speak. At this moment, an attendant came up to hold the boat. "Lose something, son?" he asked when he saw Bert's bewildered expression.

"Yes. My little brother!"

"Lost your brother!" The man looked startled. "You mean he was in the boat with you?"

Bert nodded. "He was in it up to the fire scene in the Underground City."

"Maybe he fell out!" Mrs. Bobbsey exclaimed. "We must go back and look for him!"

"Now, ma'am," the attendant said soothingly, "I'm sure the little fellow is all right. Kids often play tricks in the Underground City."

The attendant pushed a button, reversing the direction of the cable which pulled the boats.

He jumped into the two-seater with Bert, and they started back into the tunnel.

"Is your little brother particularly interested in fires?" the man asked.

"Yes, he's crazy about fire engines."

"Then that's where we'll find him," the guide said with a smile.

He was right. When they reached the row of toy buildings Freddie was sitting there on the ground in front of the display watching the entrance to the tunnel.

"Hi, Bert!" he called cheerfully. "I thought you'd come back for me."

"What's the big idea, getting out of the boat without telling me?" Bert asked sternly. "You've had everyone worried about you!"

The attendant grabbed a hook in the wall and stopped the cable. Bert helped Freddie jump into the boat, and they continued back to where their family was waiting.

"I was sure I saw Albert Garry behind those pretend buildings and you wouldn't believe me. So I decided to jump out and find him by myself," the little boy explained.

"And did you find Garry?"

"N-no, but I know I *saw* him!" Freddie declared stubbornly.

When the boat reached daylight again, the watchers looked relieved. "Freddie, you must never do such a thing again!" Mrs. Bobbsey said sternly after she had thanked the attendant.

"I'm sorry, Mother," Freddie said meekly. "I didn't mean to scare you."

Flossie felt sorry for her twin and wanted to make him happy again. "I see some big hats," she said. "Let's go over to that booth and look at them."

The group strolled over to the booth. Strings of big straw hats hung from the ends of the canopy roof. Piled on the counter were woven straw sandals, colorful beach bags, and bright scarves.

"May I have some sandals?" Nan spoke up.

The young woman behind the counter picked out a pair. "These should fit you," she said in a low, pleasant voice. "Suppose you try them on."

A little girl of about seven with short black curls sat on a stool near the end of the counter. She smiled shyly at Flossie.

"Hello," Flossie said. "I'm Flossie Bobbsey. What's your name?"

The little girl got up and walked around to the front of the counter where Nan was trying on the sandals.

"My name's Cindy Weller," she said. "This is my mommy's booth. Her name is Mrs. Peter Weller."

Nan was amazed to hear this name. Peter Weller was the name of the missing flier whom their helicopter pilot Don Wheaton had mentioned. Could he be the same person?

"Cindy, do you know a man named Don Wheaton?" she asked.

Her mother had overheard the remark and said, "Yes, we do. What made you mention him?"

"Don Wheaton brought us down here," Nan answered, not wishing to say any more.

But Cindy spoke up. "Did he tell you about my Daddy Pete? He's been away a long time."

Her mother explained that her husband, a test pilot for the International Airplane Construction Company, had disappeared while on a test flight over the ocean.

"Oh, I'm so sorry!" Flossie exclaimed, putting her arm around Cindy and hugging her.

"Maybe he'll be found," Nan said. The others expressed their sympathy too, and hoped for good news about the missing man.

"Thank you," said Mrs. Weller, whose eyes were filling with tears. Then she quickly changed the subject. "Have you been to Fairyland?"

"No," Flossie answered. "Fairyland? Where is that?"

Cindy said, "It's here in the park. I won't tell you any more about it 'cause it's a secret, but ask your mommy to take you!" The little girl's brown eyes sparkled, and she was smiling now.

Mrs. Bobbsey paid for the sandals and a beach bag she had bought, and the group started away.

"Good-by, Cindy," Flossie called. "I hope I'll see you again."

"I do, too," the little girl said.

Nan continued to talk about the missing pilot. "Oh, I hope he'll get home some day!" she said worriedly.

"We all do, dear," her mother replied, patting her daughter's shoulder affectionately.

"May we go to Fairyland?" Flossie asked.

"We really should," Dorothy spoke up. "I've been there, and it's loads of fun!"

"We'll go after lunch," the twins' mother promised.

"I want a million hot dogs and a bucket of ice cream!" Freddie announced.

Flossie giggled. "I want two million hot dogs and two buckets of strawberry ice cream!"

When they had taken their places in a small lunchroom, Freddie settled for two frankfurters and Flossie was content with one.

"What happened to that bucket of ice cream you were going to eat?" Bert asked teasingly when Freddie could finish only half his dessert.

Freddie grinned and said, "I'd be too stuffed to have fun in Fairyland!"

As the twins and their relatives walked out of the restaurant they met Officer Weaver coming in. He looked hot and tired.

"Did you find the thief?" Bert asked.

The policeman shook his head. "No," he replied. "We've gone over every inch of this park. I'm beginning to think Garry never came in here!"

When Freddie said that he had seen the thief hiding in the Underground City, the officer looked doubtful. "A couple of our men went all through that place," he said. "I don't think he could be there."

The children promised to be on the lookout for Garry and started off toward Fairyland. In the distance they could see a building which looked like a miniature castle. Flags flew from the turrets, and the sound of tinkling music could be heard.

"Ooh, isn't this 'citing?" Flossie exclaimed as they drew nearer.

In front of the castle was a small area of green grass with a white iron bench. Dorothy pointed to it.

"I've been in the castle and know the secret," she explained. "I'll sit here with Mother and Aunt Mary until you twins come out."

The four Bobbseys walked up to the little front door of the fairy castle. It was closed. But

The four Bobbseys walked up to the fairy castle

fastened to the wooden frame was a sign lettered in gold. It said:

This is the fairy's house. She invites all children to enter. If you catch the fairy, she will grant your wish.

"I hope we can catch her," Flossie exclaimed.

Nan pushed open the door. As she did, a bell tinkled. The twins walked into a little hall, with a stairway at one side. On the other side a wide doorway opened into another room.

"Let's go in there," Bert said.

The four children entered the room. It was furnished with little gold tables and chairs. There in front of the fireplace stood a beautiful fairy!

She had long yellow curls and twinkling blue eyes. Her full-skirted dress was made of a shiny, silvery material. Fastened to her shoulders were little net wings. In her hand she held a silver wand with a sparkling star at the top.

"Oh, she's bee-yoo-ti-ful!" Flossie breathed.

"I'll catch her!" Freddie called out and ran toward the fireplace.

Seeing this, the fairy raised her wand and a curtain swept across the room in front of her. Freddie dashed up and pulled the curtain to one side.

The fairy had disappeared!

CHAPTER V

A FUNNY CLUE

WHEN Flossie saw that the fairy was no longer behind the curtain she turned to Freddie. "You scared her away!" she cried, tears of disappointment coming to her eyes.

"I was only trying to catch her!" Freddie defended himself.

"Maybe she went up the chimney," Nan suggested.

Bert walked over and peered up the opening. "I don't see her, and besides there aren't any steps here."

"I guess fairies don't need steps," Flossie said sadly. "They can just make themselves invisible!"

"Let's look around the house," Nan urged. "She must be here some place."

The children wandered through the first floor. Next to the room with the fireplace was a little dining room. The table was set with pink and white dishes, and there was a bouquet of tiny roses and forget-me-nots in the center.

"How cute!" Flossie cried. She exclaimed again when she saw the kitchen. The range, refrigerator, and cupboards were built in miniature size. There were even a little clothes washer and dryer.

"Maybe the fairy's in the washing machine!" Freddie suggested with a grin.

But when Flossie opened it, she saw that it was empty. Next, they explored the second floor. Here were two little bedrooms, completely furnished with frilly white curtains at the windows and gay flowered coverlets on the beds.

The twins looked all around, under the beds and in the closets, but there was no sign of the golden-haired fairy! Sadly the children left the fairy's castle.

"Did you catch her?" Dorothy asked when her cousins came out.

They shook their heads.

"Maybe you will the next time," Dorothy said with a smile. "I had to come twice before I learned the secret."

"Oh, may we come again and try to catch the fairy?" Flossie looked pleadingly at her mother.

Mrs. Bobbsey smiled. "I'm sure we can find time," she said.

As they passed Mrs. Weller's booth Cindy ran out to meet them. She was sorry to learn that the fairy had vanished before Freddie could catch her.

"We haven't found Albert Garry either," Bert said, sighing.

"Who's he?" Cindy asked curiously.

Bert explained that the police had been looking for a thief who they thought was hiding in the park. "He's short and has light hair which sticks up on top," Bert concluded.

"I saw a man who looked like that," Cindy remarked.

"You did?" the twins chorused. "When?"

"This morning. He was running over there." Cindy pointed to the Underground City. "I thought he was funny because he was carrying a big paper shopping bag. It was white with blue stars on it! He went right past me."

"Boy!" Freddie exclaimed in excitement. "Maybe the money was in the paper bag!"

"It's a clue anyhow!" Bert agreed. "Let's tell Officer Weaver."

"There he is now," Nan started to run toward the policeman, who had stopped to get a drink at a bubble fountain.

When Nan had told her story the officer came over and questioned Cindy closely. Then he blew his whistle. Three policemen ran up from their stations in different parts of the park.

"If Garry was ever in there, he's probably gone by now," Weaver admitted, "but we can't afford to pass up any lead."

The police officers went to the ticket booth of the Underground City. After a short conversation a man came out and hung a "Closed" sign on the window.

Bert walked over to see what was happening. "Are you going to search the City again?" he asked Officer Weaver.

The policeman nodded. "Yes. We'll close the place to customers and turn on all the lights inside. That way, we ought not to miss anything."

"May I go with you?" Bert asked hopefully.

After a moment's thought, the policeman agreed. "I don't see why you shouldn't come if you want to," he said. "But keep behind me. I don't want you getting hurt."

Bert ran back to report to his mother. "All right," she said. "But be careful. Aunt Emily and I will wait for you near Mrs. Weller's booth."

The Underground City looked very different to Bert with all the lights on. He discovered that there were walks behind the scenery which faced the boats.

"These are service walks," Officer Weaver explained. "The attendants can take care of the exhibits without stepping into the water."

The four policemen walked through the Underground City, looking carefully for any sign of the thief. But they had no success.

"Well, I guess he isn't here," Officer Weaver said finally.

He stopped back at the ticket office. A man removed the "Closed" sign, and soon the boats were filling with passengers again.

While Bert had been in the Underground City with the police, the girls and Freddie had been walking around the park.

"Maybe we can find another clue to the puzzle about the robber," Freddie said hopefully.

But they saw nothing unusual. The rides were busy and the grounds full of strollers. Suddenly Nan stopped and pointed to a bench a short distance away. There, at one end, was a big paper shopping bag. It was white with blue stars on it!

"Ooh!" Flossie exclaimed. "Do you s'pose that's the money?"

"It must be!" Dorothy cried. She ran to the bench. Just as she was about to pick up the bag, the stout woman whom the girls had seen on the roller coaster waddled over from the drinking fountain.

"Would you like one of my sausages, little girl?" she asked with a big smile. "They're very

"Would you like one of my sausages, little girl?" she asked

tasty." She opened the shopping bag and pulled out a long string of frankfurters!

Dorothy blushed in confusion. "N-no, thank you," she stammered and hurried back to the other children.

"Why didn't you take a sausage?" Nan asked teasingly. Flossie and Freddie were too overcome with the giggles to say anything!

When Freddie and the girls returned to Mrs. Weller's booth they found Mrs. Bobbsey and Mrs. Minturn talking to Cindy and her mother. In a few minutes Bert joined them.

"Did the police find Albert Garry?" Nan asked eagerly.

Bert shook his head. "Not a sign of him," he replied glumly.

"Well, anyway, we've had a very exciting day at Lakeside," Aunt Emily remarked. "But it's time to leave now."

"I hope you'll come back again," Cindy said shyly.

"Yes, we're going to Fairyland," Flossie told her, "to try to catch the fairy."

"Why don't you all come Sunday?" Mrs. Weller suggested. "The Water Carnival will be held then. I think you'd enjoy it."

"I hadn't heard about that," Aunt Emily said. "What is it?"

Mrs. Weller explained that this year a carnival was to be held on the park lagoon. Children who lived along the shore would compete. "They'll decorate their boats and wear costumes, then parade through the lagoon past the judges. Prizes will be given for the most beautiful and the most original entries."

"Please, let's come and see it!" Flossie said.

"I have an idea!" Nan spoke up. "Let's enter the contest!"

CHAPTER VI

AN UNUSUAL FISH

AT NAN'S suggestion, the other children looked at one another in delight.

"Yes, let's be in the parade!" Freddie urged.

"That's a great idea!" Bert said.

"That would be fun!" Flossie and Dorothy said together.

They began to chatter excitedly about the Water Carnival. "Let's ask Hal Bingham to go in with us," Bert proposed. "Then we'll have an even number."

"Fine!" Dorothy agreed. "Hal's a good sport."

As soon as they reached Ocean Cliff the children ran over to the Bingham house. Hal was on the front porch reading.

"Hi!" he said when the Bobbseys and Dorothy came up the steps. "Guess what I got today?"

47

"What?"

"A canoe! That's why my dad took me to the city—to buy it. He says I'm old enough now to have a canoe of my own. It'll be here in a couple of days."

"That's great, Hal!" Bert said. With a grin, he added, "How about a ride in it sometime?"

"You bet! It's aluminum and will hold six people!"

"We came to ask you if you'd like to enter the Water Carnival at Lakeside with us," Nan said. She repeated what Mrs. Weller had told them about the event.

"That sounds good!" Hal said. "We can use my new canoe for one of our boats!"

"Okay. We'll see you tomorrow," Dorothy said. "Mother is expecting us home now for supper."

The conversation at the table was lively as the children related the day's adventures to Mr. Bobbsey and Uncle William.

The next morning, Bert was still thinking about Albert Garry. He telephoned Officer Weaver at police headquarters.

"I guess Garry wasn't at Lakeside after all," the officer told him. "The police in a town fifty miles up the coast are holding a man they're sure is the thief."

"I'm glad he was caught," Bert said. He was

disappointed, however, that he and the other twins had had no hand in the capture.

"A couple of our men and one of the officials from the airline have gone up there to identify him," Weaver went on. "Looks like the case is closed."

When Bert told the other children what he had learned, Nan remarked, "That mystery was certainly solved quickly!"

"I wish Daddy Pete's mystery would be solved, too," sighed Flossie.

Just then Uncle William came into the room. "How would you twins like to learn some surf casting?" he asked. "Your father and I are going down to the beach to do a little fishing."

Bert and Freddie were eager to go, and the girls said they would watch. Dorothy had often cast, with her father. All went to put on swim suits and shorts. When they arrived on the beach Uncle William was already there. The children watched as he deftly swung his pole around and sent his line whizzing out into deep water.

"Say, he's good!" Bert exclaimed admiringly.

"He sure is," Dorothy agreed proudly. "It's a lot harder to do than it looks!"

"Come on, Bert and Freddie!" called Uncle William. "I'll give you a lesson."

Bert tried first. Uncle William showed him how to hold the pole. He stood behind Bert, guided his arms around and told him when to cast. The line spun through the air but fell far short of Uncle William's mark.

"That's not bad for the first attempt!" Mr. Minturn said encouragingly. "Try again."

Bert grasped the long pole firmly with both hands and swung it back. This time when the line shot out it went farther. He pulled it in and tried once more. Finally the end of the line caught onto something.

"I think I have a bite!" Bert cried.

"Reel it in!" Uncle William advised. "Let's see what you've caught."

Steadily, Bert wound in the reel. Something dark broke the water.

"It's a black fish!" Flossie screamed, jumping up and down in excitement.

Nan ran down to the edge of the water to get a better look. Then she began to giggle. "You've snagged a piece of driftwood, Bert!" she called.

They all laughed at Bert's "fish." He grinned and handed the pole to Freddie. "It's your turn now," he said.

Uncle William showed Freddie how to hold the pole. With a determined look on his face the little boy swung it back and then snapped the pole forward.

"Oh, I have a bite!" he cried. "The first time!"

"My hair! I'm caught!" Flossie screamed

At that moment Flossie screamed. "My hair! I'm caught!"

Nan and Dorothy ran to her side. The fish-hook was snagged in Flossie's blond curls!

"Stand still, honey," Nan advised. "We'll get this untangled."

"I caught a curly fish," Freddie chuckled.

"I'm no fish, Freddie Bobbsey," Flossie said indignantly.

"I guess we'll have to wait a few years to teach you how to cast, Freddie," Uncle William said with a smile. Then he turned to Mr. Bobbsey, who had just come down to the beach. "Let's walk up the shore a little farther and fish from there," he proposed.

After the two men had gone, Dorothy made a suggestion. "You haven't had a ride behind Doodle and Dandy. I'll harness them to the cart and we can all ride to Rocky Point and look for clams."

Dorothy ran up to the house. While she was gone, Hal wandered over and decided to go along. He and Bert went up to the barn to help Dorothy harness the burros. The cart was a basket affair with seats along the sides.

In a few minutes the burros trotted smartly down a little road which led onto the hard sand. "All aboard!" called Dorothy. "There's room for everyone if we squeeze in."

Dorothy asked Bert to drive, and the boy felt very proud as he urged the burros into a trot. As the children rode along they told Hal about their adventures at Lakeside Amusement Park the day before.

"Say," he said admiringly, "you kids really ran into some excitement!"

After about a half hour's drive along the sand, Dorothy pointed straight ahead. "There's Rocky Point," she said.

The children could see a long ledge of rocks running out into the water. "The rocks are rather slippery to play on," Dorothy told them, "but the sand near them is a good place to find clams."

When they reached a wide stretch of sand, Bert halted Doodle and Dandy. The others piled out of the cart while he tied the burros to a tree which leaned out over the beach.

"Anybody hungry?" Dorothy inquired.

There was a chorus of groans from the others. "Oh, why didn't we bring something to eat?" Hal asked.

"We did!" Dorothy's blue eyes sparkled with glee. "Dinah prepared a picnic for us."

"How wonderful!" Nan exclaimed.

Dorothy went for a box she had hidden in the cart. "If you boys will build a fire, we can toast some marshmallows for dessert," she said.

While Bert, Hal, and Freddie made a little circle of stones with piled driftwood inside, the girls found long sticks to use for toasting forks. Then, when the sandwiches had been eaten, the children gathered around the fire.

"Mmm, this is dreamy!" Nan murmured later, popping a crispy-brown marshmallow into her mouth.

Freddie and Flossie had bad luck. Each dropped four marshmallows off the sticks before eating them. Some fell into the fire, the others onto the sand.

"They're meanies," declared Flossie.

Finally the twins learned to hold the sticks level until they could put the marshmallows into their mouths. In no time at all the package was gone.

"Let's hunt for clams now," Dorothy proposed. Following her instructions, the children walked along slowly near the water. Each time they spotted an air hole they quickly scooped up the wet sand around it. If there was a clam or a mussel in the handful they would drop it into the pail which Dorothy had brought. Soon the bucket was almost full.

"Maybe Dinah will make us some chowder for supper," Nan suggested. "I love chowder."

"I'm going to find some shells," Freddie announced. "Do you want to help me, Flossie?"

The small twins walked along the beach, stooping now and then to pick up a particularly pretty shell. The pockets of their shorts were soon chock-full.

"If I can find enough of these little horns, I'm going to make a necklace," Flossie said holding up a tiny purplish shell which ended in a sharp point.

She skipped along for a few minutes. Then she called out, "I've found an oyster!"

Hal ran over to her. "You're lucky. There aren't many oysters around here. Would you like me to open it for you?"

"Yes, please, I want to see the inside." Flossie handed the oyster to Hal, who drew a penknife from his pocket. The mollusk was hard to open. Several times Hal's knife slipped off the edge. But finally he got the point between the two lips and pried open the shell.

Flossie took the oyster and peered at it. Then she exclaimed, "Look, there's a little bead in it!"

"Let me see!" Nan took the oyster from her sister and examined it. A small white spot lay in the middle of the gray muscle.

"Flossie," Nan said, "you've found a pearl!"

All the children gathered around to admire Flossie's find. Then they began to look for more oysters. But no one had any luck, and finally they gave up.

"Let's look for driftwood to take home," Hal proposed.

He and Bert went up the beach. "I see a net!" Bert called presently, running toward a pile of wood and rocks.

With Hal's help he disentangled the large piece of seine which had evidently drifted in from the fishing grounds offshore.

"That's a good net," Hal said as he examined it. "Why don't you hang it in your room at home? I found one last summer and have it in my room. It looks great."

"Maybe I will," Bert agreed with enthusiasm. "Every time I look at it, I'll think of Ocean Cliff."

The boys folded up the net as well as they could, gathered pieces of driftwood, and carried them over to the cart. Freddie and Flossie were already there storing their collection of shells on the floor under the seats.

"How about going swimming?" Bert said to his little brother and sister. They agreed at once. Hurriedly pulling off their sandals, they ran down to the water's edge.

Nan stood watching intently something she had seen in the water.

"What are you looking at?" Bert asked her.

"I'm watching that brown bottle out there," his twin replied. "It's been drifting in closer to shore all the while I've been standing here."

As she spoke the bottle rolled up onto the sand on the crest of a little wave. Nan stooped and picked it up.

"Why, there's a paper inside!" she cried out excitedly.

CHAPTER VII

MESSAGE FROM THE SEA

"A PAPER!" Bert exclaimed. "Maybe it's a secret message! Let's open the bottle!"

The other children crowded around. Hal took the bottle and turned it in his hands. "The cork is sealed in," he said. "Shall we break the glass?"

"Oh, no!" Nan objected. "Let's take the bottle back and ask Dad or Uncle William to open it."

"Here they come now," Flossie called out. In a few minutes the two fathers arrived. "We thought we'd better see what you children were doing," said Mr. Bobbsey. "You've been away a good many hours."

"Did you catch any fish?" Mr. Minturn asked with a grin. "Say, what's that you're holding in your hand, Hal?"

"Nan found a secret bottle!" Flossie cried breathlessly. "Will you open it for us?"

58

Uncle William smiled and put out his hand. "Maybe you've found one of the bottles that the Hydrographic Office puts into the ocean to map the tides."

He looked the bottle over carefully. "I don't think so, though," he said. "This one hasn't been sealed with regular wax. It looks more like chewing gum!"

"Please open it, Dad!" Dorothy pleaded impatiently.

Mr. Minturn pulled a penknife from his pocket and began to dig around the edge of the cork. Little pieces of the sealing material dropped to the sand. Finally he put the point of his knife alongside the cork and began to pry it up.

The children watched, breathless with suspense. "It's coming!" Flossie cried as the cork began to move upward.

In another minute the stopper was free. Uncle William handed the bottle to Nan. "There you are!" he said with a smile.

"Hurry, Nan!" Freddie urged. "What does the paper say?"

Nan tilted the bottle and tried to shake the paper out. It would not budge. She stuck her slender finger inside and worked a few seconds until she could pull out the roll of white paper. Quickly she opened it.

"Why, the heading is International Airplane Construction Company!" she said in astonishment.

"Read what it says, Nan!" Bert begged.

Carefully Nan read:

Plane crashed. Got in raft but radio lost. Estimate longitude at 30°, latitude 40°. Anyone finding this please contact IAC.

"IAC?" Bert spoke up. "I'll bet that's International Airplane Construction—the company Captain Weller worked for! What name is signed to it?" Bert asked excitedly.

Nan passed the paper to him. "I can't make it out. The initials look like P. J., but the last name is blurred."

"I guess some water got in the bottle," Bert observed. "I can't read the last name either. Wait a minute—this note *could* be from Cindy's father. His first name begins with P—Peter!"

"I'd suggest you call the factory right away," Mr. Bobbsey advised.

The children piled into the cart and hurried home. They clustered around the phone as Nan put in the call. After a few minutes she reached the airplane factory manager and read the note to him.

There followed a short conversation, then Nan put down the receiver. She looked disappointed.

"What did he say?" Dorothy asked. "Does he think Captain Weller wrote the note?"

Nan sighed. "He didn't say. The man was very nice and thanked me for calling. But he told me they have lots of tricks like this played on them. He did say they'd investigate this bottle message thoroughly and let us know."

Nan repeated this to her father and Uncle William when they arrived. Then Bert asked, "What did you mean when you said the Hydrographic Office puts bottles into the ocean, Uncle William?"

Mr. Minturn explained that the Hydrographic Office of the Navy was interested in studying ocean currents and tide shifts. "They get officers of ships to drop bottles overboard during their voyages to all parts of the world. In these bottles are papers giving the name of the vessel and the date and position.

"Then, when a bottle is washed up on the shore, whoever finds it is asked to send the paper to the Hydrographic Office telling where and when it was found. In this way the office can figure out what tide must have carried the bottle to that spot."

"That's sure interesting!" Bert exclaimed. "Are the bottles all alike?"

"They're usually brown because the sun would burn the paper through clear glass. Also the message is written in pencil because ink is apt to dampen and spread."

"That's the reason we couldn't read the signature in the note I found!" Nan exclaimed. "It wasn't written with a pencil!"

Uncle William nodded approvingly. "That's right, Nan. And also that chewing gum didn't keep out the moisture so well as regular sealing wax would have!"

"I sure hope the note wasn't a trick," Bert said, "and that the IAC will find that pilot! But we'd better not mention any of this yet to Cindy and Mrs. Weller," he added, "until we know for sure that the one who wrote the note *is* Daddy Pete."

"That's right," Nan agreed. "We don't want to give them false hopes."

At that moment a newsboy brought the evening paper and handed it to Mr. Bobbsey. The twins' father glanced idly through it. Then all at once he exclaimed, "They haven't caught that airline thief after all! The man the police arrested in that distant town wasn't Albert Garry!"

Bert jumped up. "I'm going to call Officer Weaver and find out what happened," he declared.

He ran into the house. In a few minutes he was talking to the genial policeman. "The paper's right," the officer acknowledged. "That fellow they caught wasn't Garry although he did look like him. Garry must still be hiding in this area. Our men are watching all the roads."

"Officer Weaver," Bert said, "was the stolen money marked in any way? Could it be identified?"

There was silence at the other end of the line for a minute. Then the policeman replied, "It wasn't marked, but the airline man tells me most of it was in one-hundred-dollar bills."

"Wow!" said Bert. "That's quite a clue!" He thanked the officer and hung up.

When Bert told the other children what he had learned, Freddie became excited. "Let's go look for the money," he suggested. But at that moment Aunt Emily called them all to supper.

There was no time to follow up the new clue that evening, and at breakfast the next morning Aunt Emily said, "I'd like you children to do something for me."

"We'd love to," Nan replied. "What is it?"

"Another guest is arriving on the morning train," Mrs. Minturn said. "Will you drive the cart to the station?"

"Who's coming?" Dorothy asked eagerly.

Her mother shook her head, with a smile. "I'm not going to tell you. It's a surprise!"

When it was time to leave, Dorothy and Bert

harnessed Doodle and Dandy to the little cart, and the five children started out.

"Who do you s'pose is coming?" Flossie wondered.

"I don't know," Dorothy admitted. "But it must be someone we like. Mother always has nice surprises!"

She drove the cart into the station lot and tied the reins of the two burros to a parking meter.

"Maybe we should put in two nickels since we have two motors!" Bert suggested with a grin as he put a coin in the meter.

"Here comes the train!" Freddie cried and ran toward the station.

The other children followed and watched eagerly as the train came to a halt and the passengers began to get off.

Suddenly Bert cried, "It's Harry!"

Harry Bobbsey grinned and waved as he swung down from the train steps. All the twins greeted him warmly and Dorothy exclaimed, "It's great to see you again, Harry! Mother wouldn't tell us who was coming!"

"She telephoned my mother yesterday and invited me," Harry explained. "Of course I came right away! Things have been sort of slow on the farm since the Lakeport Bobbseys left!"

When they reached the Minturn house, the children found Hal Bingham waiting for them. "Mrs. Minturn told me Harry was arriving," he said, "so I came over to meet him."

Aunt Emily invited Hal to lunch. While eating, the twins and Dorothy told Harry about their adventures at Lakeside and the children's attempts to capture the airline thief.

"It didn't take you long to find another mystery," Harry said. "Maybe I can help you solve this one, too."

"You sure can!" Bert agreed. "Let's see if we can trace those hundred-dollar bills."

It was decided that the young detectives would walk into the shopping center and ask questions of various shopkeepers. "There can't be too many big bills like that around," Bert reasoned.

"I think it would be a good idea if Freddie and Flossie stayed here," Mrs. Bobbsey remarked.

Freddie looked disappointed for a moment. Then Flossie said, "We can build a fairy castle in the sand, Freddie. It'll be fun!"

"Okay," the little boy agreed reluctantly.

The first place the older children went to was a drugstore. When Bert asked the proprietor if anyone had changed a hundred-dollar bill there recently, the man grinned. "I haven't seen a bill like that for so long I wouldn't know what it looks like!"

Next, the children went into the hardware store next door. The manager there also said he had not taken in any such large bills. It was the same story in several more shops.

"We don't seem to be having much luck," Nan said in discouragement. "Maybe Albert Garry hasn't tried to spend any of the money yet."

"You're probably right," Bert replied. "If

we don't get a clue pretty soon, let's give it up."

The next store where they inquired was a small grocery. There was only one man in sight, and he was busy unloading some cartons and putting cans on a shelf.

"Be with you in just a minute!" he called. He took the empty carton to the back and then approached the children. "What can I do for you?" he asked pleasantly.

Bert asked his question about the hundred-dollar bill. "Why, yes," the grocer said. "A man with one was just in here. He said he didn't have any smaller bills, and when I couldn't give him change for the hundred dollars, he walked out."

"What did the man look like?" Dorothy asked eagerly.

"Well—" the grocer thought a moment— "he was sort of short and had light hair." The man glanced out the window. He pointed toward the street and exclaimed, "There he is now!"

CHAPTER VIII

PONY AND BURRO RACE

"WHERE'S the man with the hundred-dollar bill?" Nan asked excitedly, looking out the store window.

"That blond fellow going past the record shop," answered the grocer.

The children thanked him and ran from the store. Just as they reached the sidewalk, four young girls came along.

"Hi, Dorothy!"

"Hi, Hal! Where are you going so fast?"

"Can't you speak to your friends?"

The laughing youngsters forced Dorothy and Hal to stop. "Are all of you going to enter the Water Carnival contest at Lakeside Amusement Park?" one of the girls asked.

"Yes, we plan to," Dorothy answered, intending to dash on. But her friends blocked the way.

Quickly she introduced the Bobbseys, then

said. "We're in a terrible hurry. It's an important errand."

Dorothy's friends said good-by. "We'll see you all at Lakeside on Sunday!" they called as the others ran down the street.

"Oh dear!" Dorothy cried, not seeing the blond suspect. "I'm afraid we've lost that man!"

"I was watching him," said Nan. "He went in that white building at the end of the block."

"That's the library," Dorothy told her.

"Maybe he's going to hide his loot somewhere inside," Hal suggested.

The five children hurried down the street and into the library. "There he is!" Nan whispered.

A small blond man stood by the desk in the center of the room. As Bert started toward him, the man turned and looked at the children.

"Good afternoon, Dorothy," he said. "Are these your Bobbsey cousins?"

"H-hello, Mr. Crampton," Dorothy replied. "I—we thought—" Blushing, she turned to the others. "This is Mr. Crampton, a friend of Dad's."

The Bobbseys and Hal acknowledged the introduction. Then, as quickly as possible, they headed for the door again. Once outside, they all burst out laughing.

"Aren't we the good detectives, chasing Uncle William's friend?" Nan giggled.

"I almost grabbed him before he turned around," Bert confessed with a chuckle. "Wouldn't he have been surprised?"

Hal grinned. "That sure was a false clue."

"I guess it's too late to do any more sleuthing today." Dorothy sighed. "That was a good idea of yours, Bert, even if it didn't work out!"

"We'll think of something else," Bert said cheerfully. "We Bobbseys never give up!"

When Freddie and Flossie heard about the chase after Mr. Crampton, they laughed. The children were still discussing it when Hal telephoned to say that his new canoe had been delivered while he was away.

"It's a beauty! I'm calling it the *Swan*," he said. "My dad's going to take me out tomorrow and make sure I know how to manage it. I'll see you all on Saturday!"

"Come over early on Saturday," Dorothy urged. "We'll have to work on our entry for the Water Carnival."

Hal agreed and hung up.

"Cindy's coming to spend the day with us tomorrow," Flossie announced. "Aunt Emily phoned and invited her. Mrs. Weller's going to bring her in the morning."

Freddie and Flossie were waiting eagerly the next day when Mrs. Weller drove up with Cindy.

"Hurry and put on your bathing suit," Flossie said. "We're all going to play on the beach."

"We'll show you the fairy castle we built yesterday," Freddie volunteered. "We played in the sand all afternoon while the others were looking for that bad man."

"And we made a bee-yoo-ti-ful castle!" Flossie cried. "Wait till you see it!"

Cindy ran up to the girls' room and soon came down looking very pretty in a bright yellow suit.

The older children were already on the beach when the small twins and their guest arrived. Freddie looked all around.

"Why, wh-where is our castle?" he asked, bewildered.

"It must be here!" Flossie insisted, walking up the sand a little way.

"Have you lost something, honey?" Nan asked.

"Yes, our sand castle!"

Dorothy pointed to a slight hump in the sand. "Maybe that's it," she said. "I'm afraid the tide has washed most of it away!"

"Oh, our pretty castle!" Flossie looked as if she were about to cry.

Cindy came to the rescue. "Let's make another one," she proposed.

"Sure," Freddie agreed. "We can build a bigger one this time!"

The three set to work. When Dinah called them to lunch they had almost finished the castle. This time they had built it far up on the beach so it could not be washed away.

"I don't think the tide will ever come up this far," Freddie said hopefully.

The children dressed quickly and soon met in the cool dining room. They chattered busily as they ate chicken salad and potato chips. Then Dinah brought in a big coconut cake.

Cindy's eyes sparkled. "This is the nicest time I've had for ages!" she announced happily.

"How would you like to ride in a burro cart this afternoon?" Dorothy inquired.

"Oh, yes!" Flossie cried. "You'll love Doodle and Dandy!"

Cindy was interested to hear about the little burros and eager to take a ride in the basket cart. Freddie decided that he would rather go back to the beach and finish the sand castle.

Bert and Harry said they had other plans. So only Nan and Dorothy and the two little girls started off in the burro cart.

"This is fun!" Cindy exclaimed as the two little animals trotted along the hard sand.

Just then another cart, pulled by a pony, turned onto the beach ahead.

"There's Nancy Bowden," Dorothy said. "Hi!" she called.

The other girl, who was about Dorothy's age but smaller, waved. She reined in her pony and waited until Doodle and Dandy caught up. Dorothy introduced her to Nan, Flossie, and Cindy.

"Can your pony run as fast as Dorothy's burros?" Flossie asked.

Nancy's eyes twinkled. "Want to race and find out?" she inquired.

"We have a bigger load than you have!" Dorothy protested.

"But you have two animals," said Nancy. "That makes up for the extra weight."

Dorothy looked at Nan. "Shall we?" she asked.

"Sure!" Nan agreed. "It'll be fun!"

"Okay," Dorothy said to Nancy. "How far shall we make it?"

Nancy shaded her eyes and peered down the beach. "See that dead tree at the edge of the sand?" she asked. "We'll make that the finish line. The first one who passes it wins the race!"

"Right!" Dorothy said. She straightened in her seat and took a firm grip on the reins. "When Nan yells, 'ready, get set, go,' we'll start!"

Nan waited until Cindy had taken her position, then gave the signal. "Giddap!" Dorothy and Nancy shouted. The burros and pony began to trot down the sand.

"Oh, she's beating us!" Flossie cried as the pony cart quickly pulled ahead.

"Come on, Doodle! Come on, Dandy!" Dorothy called, slapping the reins on the burros' backs.

"We're gaining!" Cindy called as she clung to the side of the basket cart.

The burros suddenly realized they were in a

race. They ran faster and faster, their long ears flattened against their heads. The pony also dashed along, his little hoofs kicking up the sand.

They were really racing now. The two carts careened wildly up the beach, while the children hung on as tightly as they could

"Whoa!" Dorothy cried.

"Whoa!" screamed Nancy.

Dorothy's cart was on the inside. When it passed the dead tree which marked the finish line one wheel struck the wood. Flossie lost her grip and flew over the side!

Nan grabbed the reins and helped Dorothy bring the excited burros to a stop. Nancy had managed to halt her pony. The children all jumped out and ran back to where Flossie sat on the sand.

"Are you hurt, honey?" Nan asked anxiously, bending down beside her little sister.

"N-no." Flossie smiled up at Nan. "But I sat down awful hard!"

"Well, you won the race anyhow," Nancy said with a grin. "I guess two burros are better than one pony!"

She and Dorothy turned their carts around and drove back slowly. Flossie began to tell Cindy about their picnic at Rocky Point, two days earlier.

"Nan found a bottle with a note from a lost man. The initials were P. J.," Flossie said.

Nan turned and gave her sister a warning glance.

"Oh!" Flossie gasped. "I forgot—I wasn't s'posed to tell!"

"P. J.!" Cindy cried excitedly. "Those are my daddy's initials! They stand for Peter John. Maybe the note was from him!" The little girl begged to hear more about the Bobbseys' discovery.

Nan finally explained that the paper had been from International Airplane Construction and that she had phoned them. "They're going to investigate," she said.

"Oh, Cindy!" Flossie cried. "Wouldn't it be wonderful if the note was from your daddy?"

By this time they had reached the Minturns' house. The girls all waved good-by to Nancy as Dorothy turned the cart into the roadway.

Mrs. Bobbsey and Mrs. Minturn were on the porch as the children came from the barn. "We have good news for you," Aunt Emily called out.

"Has Albert Garry been caught?" Nan asked.

Aunt Emily shook her head, "Not that. A man from IAC called and wanted to talk to you. He said to tell you they have checked into the location given in that note you found. They feel it's quite possible the note was written by Captain Weller! They are sending out a search plane immediately."

Cindy's face lighted up. "My daddy is alive!" she cried.

Mrs. Bobbsey and Nan and Flossie looked at one another. They hoped the little girl was not wrong. But the note had been written two months ago. Was the pilot still all right?

Cindy looked up at Mrs. Bobbsey, her face still aglow. "I *know* Daddy Pete is safe!" she said.

CHAPTER IX

THE RESCUE COW

NAN ran over to hug Cindy. "I'm sure your father is safe, too!" she said.

Cindy turned to Aunt Emily. "I've had a lovely time," she said, "but please may I go home now? I want to tell Mother about Daddy Pete."

While all this excitement was going on at Ocean Cliff, Bert and Harry were having an adventure of their own. On the beach that morning Bert had said in a low voice to Harry, "See those woods on the other side of the highway?"

Harry had looked toward the distant trees and nodded. "Yes. Why?"

"Well, I think that thief Garry might be hiding in there. How about our taking a walk in the woods this afternoon and looking around?"

"Okay," Harry agreed enthusiastically. "Dorothy says Indians roamed in there a long time ago. Maybe we can find some arrowheads." Harry had a collection of Indian relics which he had dug up when the fields on his father's farm had been plowed.

After the girls had gone out in the donkey cart and Freddie had returned to the beach, Bert and Harry set off for the woods.

"It's swell and cool in here," Harry commented as the two boys made their way among the trees.

"Yes, and it sure would be a good place to hide," Bert replied. "Let's keep our eyes open for any sign that Garry might have camped here."

The boys walked along slowly, peering right and left. The road was out of sight now, and the noise of traffic had faded away.

Suddenly Bert's foot hit something. He bent down and picked up a small stone. "Hey, look at this!" he called to Harry. "Do you think it's an arrowhead?"

Harry took the stone and examined it. It was heart-shaped with sharp edges and point. "I'm sure it is!" he said. "Let's see if we can find some more!"

Bert and Harry got down on their knees to search among the brown pine needles for more arrowheads. "Here's another!" Harry cried out in a few minutes. He held up an odd-shaped stone with many dents in it.

"It doesn't look like the first one we found," Bert remarked.

"I know," Harry replied, "but I found one like this on the farm, and Dad said it was Indian!"

The boys were so interested in looking for more Indian relics that they forgot they had come into the woods to search for the thief. Finally, when they had collected a pocketful of arrowheads, Bert looked up.

"Say, it's getting dark in here! We'd better find our way out now while we can still see!" he said. "We came in this way, didn't we?"

Bert turned to his right and began to walk briskly.

Harry followed for a few minutes, then stopped. "I think we're going in the wrong direction, Bert. This doesn't look right."

Bert looked up among the tall trees. "We should be able to tell by the sun, but it must have become cloudy. I can't see it!"

The boys walked on for a few minutes, then stopped again. "I guess we really are lost!" Bert admitted.

"What do we do now?" Harry asked uncertainly.

"I suppose we can build a signal fire," Bert suggested. "Maybe someone will see it."

"Ssh!" Harry held up his hand. "I hear someone coming! Maybe it's Garry!"

They listened. There came the sound of crackling branches. Something was moving in their direction through the underbrush. But the steps did not sound as if they were being made by a human being!

"D-do you think there are any bears in here?" Bert asked, his voice a little shaky.

The boys waited, their hearts pounding. Then, suddenly, a large animal broke through the bushes in front of them.

"A cow!" Harry cried with glee. "A nice old bossy!"

Bert laughed. "She sure had me scared!"

"If we follow her, she'll lead us out of the woods," Harry said. "Go on, Bossy!" he urged, giving the cow a light slap on the flank.

The animal flicked her tail and slowly pushed her way through the underbrush. Bert and Harry followed. In a few minutes the cow had made her way to the edge of the woods.

"We weren't very far in, but we were going the wrong way," Bert observed.

When the boys and the cow emerged from the woods a woman ran toward them from a farmhouse nearby. "Oh, you've found Daisy!" she said thankfully. "My husband has just gone to look for her."

Bert grinned. "We didn't exactly find Daisy," he explained. "She found us!" He told how he and Harry had been lost in the woods.

"I always said Daisy was smart!" the woman said. "You boys come in the house, and I'll give you some milk and cookies. You must be hungry!"

After the boys had finished two glasses of the creamy milk apiece and each eaten a half dozen crisp cookies, they thanked the farmer's wife. She told them how to reach Ocean Cliff, and they left.

That evening the children had a great deal to talk about. First, Flossie had to tell the boys about the exciting race on the sand and how she had fallen out of the cart. Then Nan and Dorothy told about the call from the airplane company.

"Cindy is sure her father will be found," Nan concluded happily.

The boys described their expedition into the woods. "We had a very dangerous time!" Harry said. "We were almost eaten by a bear—only it turned out to be a cow!"

The others laughed heartily at the idea of Bert and Harry being scared by a cow. Later when Bert was standing on the porch looking out over the water, Dorothy crept up behind him and gave a low *moooo!* Nan did the same thing to Harry a few minutes later.

"All right!" Bert said. "You girls think you're funny, but we'll get even with you!"

The next morning Bert and Harry put on their swim trunks and hurried down to the beach.

"We may as well go, too," Dorothy said, and

the three girls went upstairs to their room to change. Then as they started to get into their bathing suits Flossie cried, "I can't get my foot into the leg of my suit!"

"My suit is sewed up all around!" Nan exclaimed.

"So is mine." Dorothy giggled. "And I'll bet I know who did it, too! Bert or Harry!"

Nan was busy with scissors cutting open Flossie's and her suits. "Someone must have helped them! Bert can't sew!" she declared.

"Would Dinah, do you think?" Dorothy suggested.

Flossie pulled on her suit and ran down to the kitchen. "Dinah," she said, "did you help the boys sew up our suits?"

A big smile spread over the cook's face. "Now, honey," she said, "why would I do a thing like that?" She turned away chuckling.

Nan, who had followed Flossie into the room, smiled. "You act guilty to me, Dinah," she said teasingly. "We'll think up something to get even with the boys, and you'll have to help us!"

Dinah shook with laughter. "You can count on me, honey," she promised.

When the girls reached the beach a little later, Harry commented, "It took you a long time to get ready, didn't it?"

"Oh, no," Nan replied with an innocent air.

"We were just talking to Dinah!" None of the girls mentioned the sewn-up suits, and the boys looked baffled.

After lunch Hal came over to the Minturns. "Sorry I couldn't get here this morning," he told the children, "but my mother had some errands for me to do. How about the Water Carnival tomorrow? Have you planned anything?"

"Let's be Indians," Harry suggested. "It would be easy. We could wear brown swim trunks and paint our faces."

"And we can use my new canoe!" Hal joined in.

"I know what else we can use if Aunt Emily doesn't mind!" Bert exclaimed. He ran into the kitchen and in a few minutes returned with a feather duster.

"Aunt Emily says she doesn't need it and we can tear it up if we want," Bert reported. The boys decided to make headbands with feathers.

"If you fellows are Indians, why don't we be pioneers in the West?" Dorothy said. "We can fix up our outboard motorboat to look like a covered wagon. And we have a trunk full of old-fashioned clothes in the attic!"

Hal and Harry hurried over to the shopping center to get their hair bands and some grease paint for their faces. Bert said he would go to the lake with Dorothy and Nan to help them trim the *Firefly*. They took some loops of wire from the barn and made a frame for the wagon roof.

"What can we use for the cover?" Nan asked.

"How about some old white beach towels?" Dorothy said.

She hurried off to get the towels, and they were draped over the wire. The children stood back to admire their work.

"It looks great!" Bert said. "But I'll bet it's the only covered wagon that ever had a motor!"

Back at the house Nan and Dorothy found long, full skirts and shawls for themselves and a little white dress and sunbonnet for Flossie.

"You sure look like old-time western movies," Bert commented.

By this time Harry and Hal had returned with their purchases. "Come on," Dorothy directed. "Let's get into our costumes and have a dress rehearsal!"

A few minutes later, all the children gathered on the front porch. "How do we look, Mother?" Flossie asked, holding out her skirt and whirling around.

"Wonderful!" Mrs. Bobbsey said. "If you'll come out in back, where the light is better, I'll take your pictures."

As they posed for the snapshots Mrs. Bobbsey

said, "Goodness, that line full of clothes will be in the picture. Nan, run in and ask Dinah to take them down, please. They're dry."

As Nan went off, Freddie suddenly said, "Everyone is in the carnival except Snoop! Can't he do something?"

The other children laughed. What could a cat do in a water carnival?

But Freddie was serious. "I know," he said. "Snoop can be a black panther that the Indians have just shot! I'll sling him over my shoulder the way they do in the movies!"

Flossie giggled at the thought of Snoop being a panther as her twin ran off to find his pet. Snoop was asleep in the shade of the barn and did not want to be carried away.

While he was being arranged on Indian Bert's shoulder, Dinah came out to the yard with her clothes basket. She took the dry clothes from the line and stood aside to watch the picture-taking.

"You all look mighty nice," she commented.

"Thank you," said Nan. "We're ready, Mother!" she called, as Bert held Snoop steady on his shoulder.

When Mrs. Bobbsey had the camera focused Bert took his hand away. At that moment Snoop gave a great leap and landed *thump* on top of the laundry in Dinah's basket!

CHAPTER X

THE PANTHER'S BATH

"OH, MY!" Dinah yelled. She dropped the basket, spilling the clothes onto the grass.

Snoop crawled from the basket, a red sock draped over his black head! He gave a hurried look around, then streaked for the barn.

The children doubled over with laughter. Even Mrs. Bobbsey had difficulty keeping her face straight as she said to Dinah, "I'm sorry Snoop did that. We'll help you pick up the laundry."

By this time Dinah had recovered from her surprise and began to chuckle. "That Snoop!" she said. "He's sure got more tricks than any cat I ever saw!"

Nan and Dorothy collected the scattered laundry. "I guess nothing got dirty, Dinah," Nan said comfortingly as they filled the basket.

Still chuckling, Dinah carried it into the

house. Freddie, meanwhile, had run after the cat.

"Snoop says he'll be good," the little boy announced when he returned with the pet in his arms. "He was just scared."

"Panthers aren't s'posed to be scared!" Flossie said with a giggle.

Snoop did seem to be sorry for the commotion he had caused and lay quietly on Bert's shoulder while Mrs. Bobbsey took their pictures.

Then Hal said good-by. "See you after lunch tomorrow!" he called as he left.

The next day was bright and clear. After church and a quick lunch the children got dressed for the Carnival and went to Lakeside, carrying Snoop in a basket.

Hal beached his canoe next to the outboard motor covered wagon. On the side of the silvery craft the words *The Swan* were painted in red. Hal's face was painted with streaks of red, yellow, and green. He wore swim trunks and several strings of bright-colored beads about his neck. Stuck in the back of his red headband were feathers from the duster.

"Ooh!" Flossie cried. "You look awful scary!"

Bert and Freddie, dressed like Hal, clapped their hands to their mouths and uttered Indian war cries.

Hal beached his canoe next to the outboard motor
covered wagon

"Heap big chief scalp little girl!" Bert shouted and grabbed Flossie's yellow curls. Flossie screamed in pretended terror.

The boys started off in the canoe with Hal and Bert at the paddles. The girls followed in the boat.

When they arrived at the lagoon, it was packed with boats and children in costume. Hal and Dorothy tied up their craft, and the children all jumped out onto the little dock.

Cindy Weller was waiting for them. "Oh, you all look so nice," she said, then explained, "You have to go up to that desk and register."

"Is there any news about your father?" Nan asked quickly.

Cindy shook her black curls. "The IAC man called Mother and told her they were sending out a plane to look for Daddy Pete, but we haven't heard anything more."

"I'm sure they'll find him," Nan said kindly.

At the registration desk Flossie looked at Bert. "Where's Snoop?" she asked. "Doesn't he have to register?"

Bert grinned. "He was asleep in the bottom of the canoe, so we decided not to disturb him. We'll register for Snoop."

The children listened carefully to the rules and instructions for the contestants, then started back to the boats. "We'll see you when the parade is over!" Flossie called to Cindy.

Suddenly Hal's voice was heard above the chattering of the crowd. "My canoe's gone!"

Nan, Flossie, and Dorothy ran to the spot where Hal and the other boys stood staring at the empty space where the canoe had been.

"Who could have taken it?" Dorothy asked in bewilderment.

"And Snoop's in it!" Freddie cried. "Snoop's been stolen!"

In a few minutes a crowd had gathered at the place where the boats were tied up. As Hal was questioning the bystanders, a man pushed his way through.

"That aluminum canoe tied here?" he said to Hal. "Was that yours?"

The boy nodded.

"About ten minutes ago," the newcomer said, "I saw a man jump into it and paddle away. I noticed him because I thought I had seen some children arrive in that same canoe."

"Thank you, sir," said Bert. "Did you see which way he went?"

"Yes, I watched him," the man replied. "He paddled down to the end of the lagoon, then turned north into the lake."

"Come on, Hal, let's follow him!" Bert cried. "May we take your boat, Dorothy?"

"Sure, go ahead!" Dorothy said. "Good luck! I hope you catch him."

Bert, Harry, and Hal jumped into the boat. Bert started the motor and turned the bow toward the open water. When they reached the main part of the lake, he turned north.

"It's going to be hard to find anyone along here," Hall observed. "There are so many coves, a man could pull into one and we'd miss him completely!"

"Remember, though, he's paddling and we have a motor," Bert reminded Hal. "I think we can catch up to him."

The boys were silent for a while as the motorboat put-putted up the lake. They scanned the shoreline intently, searching for a sign of Hal's aluminum canoe.

"It looks as if the thief has given us the slip," Harry observed finally.

Several times Hal thought he saw the canoe in the underbrush which grew down to the water's edge. But when Bert brought the *Firefly* closer to shore, it generally proved to be only the trunk of a dead tree which had fallen among the bushes.

Then suddenly Bert shouted and pointed to a little cove they were just passing. "Isn't that a canoe on the sand in there?" he asked.

Hal shaded his eyes and peered at the spot. "Turn around!" he cried. "I think you're right!"

Deftly, Bert turned the boat in a wide circle and headed toward the little cove. He ran his craft up on the shore next to the canoe. It was *The Swan!*

"Wow! Am I lucky!" Hal said.

"I hope Snoop's still there!" Bert exclaimed.

He and Harry jumped into the water and waded to the spot where the canoe was beached. They looked in and began to laugh.

There was Snoop sound asleep in his basket in the bottom of the canoe! Bert bent over and tickled the cat under the chin.

"Wake up, Snoop, old boy!" he said. "Time to go back to the Water Carnival!"

The cat stretched and sat up. "Say, what's that in back of the basket?" Harry asked. He leaned over and picked up a white cloth cap. On the visor was some faded printing. Hal came up, and the trio studied the letters.

"This could be the thief's cap!" Bert said, and spelled out: *"ed Cargo."*

"Yes," Harry agreed. "But it doesn't sound like a person's name."

Bert frowned, concentrating. Then he burst out, "I know—the first two letters are only part of a word. The full name on the cap could have been Allied Cargo Airlines—the company Albert Garry worked for!"

Harry excitedly agreed. "Sure!" he cried. "Garry was the one who stole your canoe, Hal!"

"He's probably been hiding in the amusement park ever since last Tuesday!" Bert added. "And the carnival today gave him a good chance to steal the canoe for his getaway!"

"Maybe we can still catch him!" Hal said in excitement. "He can't have gone very far."

Quickly the boys scanned the area for any sign of the suspected thief. Suddenly Bert shouted:

"I see footprints!" He led the way to deep shoe tracks in the sand.

"Oh boy!" Hal exclaimed. "Let's follow them. They *could* belong to Garry."

Harry also was eager to pursue the trail of footprints. But Bert looked sober.

"I wish we could follow the prints and find Garry," he said, "but we ought to get back to the park. We have Dorothy's boat, and the girls can't enter the contest without it."

"That's right," Hal agreed. "Harry and I'll paddle the canoe back while you go in the covered wagon!" he ended with a grin. "That way we'll make better time!"

Harry and Hal paddled as fast as they could and drew up at the Lakeside dock not long after

Bert. When they arrived they saw the Bobbsey boy deep in conversation with a policeman.

As they came up the officer turned to them. "Bert tells me that you think Garry stole your canoe and escaped. I'll send a prowl car out to look for him."

Then the officer continued with a rueful grin, "To think that crook has been hiding out here for almost a week and none of us could catch him!"

At that moment an announcement came over the loudspeaker, asking all entries to line up at the end of the lagoon for the parade past the judges' stand.

A band began to play as the entries took their places. The boat with Nan, Flossie, and Dorothy was third in line, while the boys' canoe was next to last.

All the children admired the first boat in line. It had a great paper dragon riding in it. The giant head was lighted from inside by an electric lantern which was fixed to go on and off at intervals. This made the dragon look as if it were spouting fire.

"Ooh! It looks real!" Flossie cried, shivering a little.

The next boat held two boys dressed as clowns. They were pretending to have a boxing match with huge gloves made of balloons.

"Oh, look!" Nan laughed. "There's Washington crossing the Delaware!" She pointed to a rowboat filled with boys dressed as Revolutionary soldiers. In the center, with his foot up on one of the seats and one arm pointing forward, was "George Washington"!

Another boat carried several pretty girls in bathing suits who tossed a big beach ball back and forth.

Slowly the parade moved past the reviewing stand. Just before the boys' turn came, Snoop began to squirm on Bert's shoulder.

"Here, Freddie, take your black panther!" Bert said, passing the cat down to the little boy. "Maybe you can make him stay still!"

As the Indian canoe slipped past the judges, a wave of laughter swept over the watching crowd. Snoop was seated on Freddie's shoulder calmly giving himself a bath!

When the parade was over the boats lined up along the side of the lagoon while the judges conferred. Everyone waited eagerly to hear who had won the prizes. The three men who were doing the judging walked along and examined the boats closely.

Finally they seemed to have made their decision. There was a flourish from the band, and the head judge stood up.

After announcing that the first prize would

go to the paper dragon as the most original, he said, "The second prize for the boat entry showing the most ingenuity goes to Dorothy Minturn and Nan and Flossie Bobbsey."

There was loud applause. Then the judge held up his hand. "We have decided to award an extra prize today," he said.

A hush fell over the crowd as they waited for the announcement.

CHAPTER XI

A FLOATING TRICK

"THE third prize," said the judge, "goes to the one who gave us the biggest laugh—Freddie Bobbsey and his black panther Snoop!"

Freddie grinned at the announcement that he and Snoop had won a prize. "I'm sorry Snoop wouldn't play dead," he said to Bert, "but I guess the judges liked him anyway!"

The band struck up another lively tune as the winning boats swung around to the judges' stand to receive their prizes. The designers of the fiery dragon won sets of flippers, face masks, and snorkel tubes.

The girls' prize was an inflatable rubber raft with paddles. "We can have a lot of fun with this!" Dorothy exclaimed after they had thanked the judges and moved away.

Hal held his canoe steady while Freddie leaned forward to take his prize from the head judge. It was a large toy sailboat with three masts and several sails.

Freddie's eyes shone with happiness. "Thank you!" he cried. "She's a beauty!"

That night as the girls were talking about the carnival before going to sleep, Dorothy suddenly sat up in bed. "You know, we've never done anything to get even with Bert and Harry for sewing up our swim suits!"

"That's right!" Nan said. "What can we do?"

There was silence for a moment, then Dorothy giggled. "I have an idea," she said.

When she told Nan and Flossie her plan, they too laughed. "That's good, Dorothy," Nan said. "I'm sure Dinah will help us."

After breakfast the next morning, Bert and Harry wandered out to the porch while the girls went into the kitchen.

"Dinah," Flossie said, "remember, you said you'd help us play a trick on the boys?"

"I sure will, honey," the cook said. "What you all got in mind?"

The girls told her what they needed. In a few minutes the articles were collected and they went to work. Finally Dorothy stood up and started toward the door.

"Come on!" she said. "I think that's all we can do. I hope it works!"

Nan and Flossie followed their cousin upstairs and they got into their bathing suits. When they went out onto the porch, Bert pointed to a yellow rubber boat.

"We blew up your raft for you," he said. "Harry and I'll get on our trunks, then we can try it out!"

While the boys were upstairs, Nan, Flossie, and Dorothy ran down to the sand. "I'll hide it here by this driftwood," Dorothy said, putting something down and covering it with sand.

By the time Bert and Harry reached the beach the girls were already pulling the raft out onto the water. For the next half hour the six children played with the rubber boat. Bert took Freddie and Flossie for a ride in it. Then the others took turns paddling around.

Finally, tired out, they all flopped down on the sand. Dorothy took a seat near the pile of driftwood. In a few minutes she stood up.

"I'm going in again and get a little of this sand off," she said. As Dorothy walked past Nan she winked.

Dorothy waded out until the waves splashed over her shoulders, then came in and sat down by Bert. He and Harry were busy discussing the events of the day before.

"I think we ought to go back up there where we found Hal's canoe," Bert said. "We might—" He stopped, his attention caught by something bobbing in the water. "Say! That looks like another bottle!"

Bert got up hurriedly and ran down to the water's edge. He waded out a short distance then turned around triumphantly, a brown bottle held high in his hand.

"I've found one!" he exclaimed. "Maybe it's another message from Captain Weller!"

All the children jumped to their feet. Harry was particularly excited. "I'm glad I'm here," he said. "I missed seeing the one Nan found."

Bert had been examining the bottle. "I think it's one of those from the Hydrographic Office," he said excitedly. "See, it has real sealing wax around the cork!"

"Why don't you open it, Bert?" Flossie cried impatiently, her blue eyes snapping with mischief.

"Okay." Bert looked around. "Maybe I can get the seal off with this." He picked up a sharp shell and began to chip off the wax.

Finally it came loose, revealing the cork which stuck up slightly from the neck of the bottle. Using the sharp point of another shell, Bert managed to pry it out.

"Hurry! Hurry!" Freddie urged.

Eagerly Bert pushed his finger into the bottle and worked out a rolled-up piece of paper.

"What does it say?" Harry asked.

Bert's face was a study in bewilderment as he read the message:

Help! I'm drowning!
Moby Dick, the Whale.

At the sound of laughter from Dorothy, Nan, and Flossie, Bert looked up. "So that's it!" he said with a grin. "Just you wait!"

The girls were still laughing at the success of their trick when Hal came over after lunch. "Did you know that Bert found another floating bottle this morning?" Dorothy greeted him.

"Nan and Dorothy think they're very clever," Bert said with a sheepish grin. "I'll get even with them!"

Hal laughed. "How about running up a white flag of truce? Come with me to the cove where we found the canoe yesterday. That fellow Garry hasn't been caught yet."

"Sounds great!" Bert said. "We can follow those footprints and maybe find a clue to that thief."

Nan, Dorothy, and Harry were eager to go too. But Freddie and Flossie decided they would rather stay at home and sail the new toy boat.

"May I paddle, Hal?" Dorothy asked hopefully. "I'd like to see how your canoe handles."

"Sure, get in the bow," Hal replied as he walked back to the stern.

When the others were seated, Dorothy gave the silvery craft a push and jumped in. Then, with strong, even strokes, she and Hal paddled the canoe up the lake. In a few minutes they had passed the water carnival area.

"It was about the fourth or fifth cove above here, wasn't it?" Hal called up to the two boys in the center.

They both nodded. Everyone was quiet for a while as the children peered into each little inlet they passed.

"There!" Bert cried. "I think it was this one."

Dorothy and Hal turned the canoe and headed for the shore. "You're right!" Hal called. "I see where Garry beached."

When the canoe touched the shore Dorothy leaped out and held the craft while the others walked forward and got out. Then they pulled the canoe up onto the narrow, sandy beach.

"I hope no one's rubbed out the footprints," Harry said worriedly.

"Are these the same ones you saw?" Dorothy pointed to deep marks in the sand, leading away from the water.

"Yes," replied Bert, and ran on ahead, following the shoe tracks. When he reached the spot where the sand ended, Bert cried, "There's a path here!"

A narrow lane ran from the beach through

the low underbrush. The ground was marshy and the path was muddy. The footprints were easily traced. The children followed them until they reached the highway which ran parallel to the ocean.

"Which way now?" Hal asked as they all paused by the side of the road.

"He could have gone in either direction from here," Nan said, in discouragement. "Or a car might have picked him up."

"Maybe he crossed the road." Bert ran to the other side of the highway and peered carefully around. "Can't make out anything here," he said sadly.

"We may as well go back to the lake," Dorothy said after Bert joined them again.

The children walked back across the stretch of land between the highway and the lake. Nan, who had knotted her favorite red scarf around her neck, took it off and trailed it from one hand.

Suddenly she felt a tug on the scarf which pulled her backwards. "Oh!" she screamed, looking down. "It's a huge turtle!"

Hal ran to her side. "Watch out!" he warned. "He's a snapper! Better let go of the scarf!" Quickly Nan dropped it.

The turtle was about a foot long. He had a grayish brown shell with regular, square-

shaped markings. His little head with beady
eyes protruded some distance from the shell.

"I'll see if I can rescue your scarf," Hal said.

"Oh, let it go!" Nan said with a shiver. "He
might hurt you!"

"Snapping turtles are rather dangerous," Hal
admitted, "but maybe I can fool him!" The boy
picked up a stick and prodded the creature's
long neck.

Immediately the turtle let go of the scarf and grabbed the stick. Then he waddled awkwardly away. The children stood still until they saw him slide into the lake.

"That's funny," Harry remarked. "We find turtles on our farm and they always pull their heads and tails in under the shell when they see anyone."

"Those are probably box turtles," Hal explained. "A snapping turtle's head is too big to get under the shell. This one must have been out looking for something different to eat. They don't usually get very far away from the water."

"You seem to know a lot about turtles, Hal," Nan said admiringly.

"I've read a bit about them," the boy replied, picking up Nan's scarf and handing it to her. "That large upper shell is called the carapace and the bottom shell the plastron. You'd be surprised at the different markings on turtles' shells."

"Turtles are fun," Dorothy joined in. "I've had them for pets. Some of them will even eat from your hand!"

"That's right," Hal agreed. "You just happened to run into the mean type, Nan. Most of them are harmless."

"Well, if you think Nan's friend is safely in the water," Bert said with a grin, "let's see if we can discover anything on the lake shore."

The children walked along the edge of the lake a short distance in both directions from the spot where Hal's canoe had been found. They scanned the ground carefully, but found nothing unusual. Finally they turned back to the canoe.

As Harry started to step into the craft a small piece of paper at the edge of the water caught his eye. He bent down and picked it up. Then he called to the others, "Look at this!"

Bert ran up and took the paper. "Why," he cried, "it's a ticket to the Underground City!"

CHAPTER XII

RUNAWAY SAILBOAT

"THE Underground City!" the others echoed.

"Yes," Bert replied. "I guess Freddie was right when he said he saw Garry in there."

"Let's take this to the police," Nan suggested. "It's more evidence that Albert Garry was here."

The children piled into the canoe again. This time they did not stay along the shore but paddled in a straight line toward Ocean Cliff. When they reached police headquarters they were glad to find their friend Officer Weaver at the desk.

"Well, well, here are the young detectives!" he said cheerily. "Any more clues for us? We still haven't been able to put our hands on that airline thief!"

When Bert gave him the ticket which Harry had found, the police officer said, "Garry *must* be hanging out in that park. But we've searched every inch of it without finding him! I'll put a special plainclothes guard at the entrance to the Underground City in case he tries to get in there."

He thanked the children for their help, then they went home. All the grownups were away except Dinah. Nan asked her where Freddie and Flossie were.

"Some neighbor took 'em over to the lake to sail that boat Freddie won," the cook replied.

At this moment the phone rang. Bert answered it. "What!" he exclaimed. "Yes, we'll be right over!"

Bert ran to the others. "Freddie and Flossie have disappeared! That was Mrs. Smith, who took them to the lake. She left them for a few minutes to go for some ice cream. When she came back, they were gone!"

The five children dashed from the house and raced toward the lake.

An hour before this, Freddie and Flossie had been playing contentedly in a little cove on the lake shore with Mrs. Smith watching them.

The breeze had been coming from just the right direction. It filled the sails of the toy boat and sent it flying across the narrow strip of water that formed the cove.

"It's a fast boat!" Freddie said proudly. He

ran along the shore and picked it up when it touched land.

Then Flossie had a turn at launching the miniature craft. After they had sent the boat across the cove several times, Flossie suggested they play water carnival.

"How can we do that when there aren't any other boats?" Freddie objected.

"We could dress this one up," Flossie insisted.

"How?"

"With flowers and leaves and things," Flossie replied.

"Okay."

Freddie put the boat on the ground and helped his twin collect a few wildflowers and some trailing vines. Mrs. Smith said, "While you're doing that, I'll get ice cream for all of us. You'd like some, wouldn't you?"

"Oh, yes, thank you," the twins answered, and she hurried off to the amusement park to make the purchase.

Flossie and Freddie wound the trailing vines around the masts and put the flowers on the deck.

"There! The boat looks bee-yoo-ti-ful!" Flossie cried, as she set the little craft in the water again.

While the children had been gathering the flowers, the wind had changed. Now, instead of sailing across the cove, the boat headed out into the lake.

"Oh, stop it, Freddie!" Flossie shouted.

"I can't!" Freddie answered in distress. "It's too far out!"

The little boat sailed farther and farther away from the shore. Freddie looked around in desperation.

A short distance up the shore he saw a small rowboat tied to a dock. Freddie ran toward it.

"We can borrow this," he called back to his twin.

"Oh, I don't think we should!" Flossie objected. "Besides, you can't row!"

"Sure I can!" Freddie replied. "It's not hard!"

"We-ell," said Flossie doubtfully. "I guess we'll have to take the boat if we want to rescue your prize."

Freddie climbed in and took the middle seat. "Take that rope off the pole," he directed. "Then we can go."

Flossie untied the rope, then sat down timidly, facing Freddie. The little boy put his hands on the oars and began to row.

"You watch the sailboat, Flossie!" he said, "and tell me when we get close to it."

"It's going awfully fast," Flossie reported. "You'll have to hurry to catch it!"

Freddie tried to row faster, but the oars were too heavy for him. As he gave a hard pull on one oar it skimmed the water, splashing Flossie from head to toe.

"Oh, Freddie!" she protested. "You don't know how to row at all!"

"I do so!" he said. But the next minute he dug the oars too deeply into the water. They flew from his hands and one struck him on the chest. He fell backward off the seat into the bottom of the rowboat! The oars had unlocked and started to float away.

"Oh, Freddie," said Flossie, her lip trembling. "Are you hurt?"

Freddie struggled back onto the seat. "I'm all right." He tried to reach the oars, but they were too far away.

"Maybe we could just paddle with our hands," Flossie suggested. "You paddle on one side and I'll take the other."

This did not work either. The boat moved quietly along, blown by the brisk wind.

"Can you see the sailboat?" Freddie asked.

"Yes, but we're not getting very near it," Flossie replied. "Maybe we should go back."

"Not until we get my prize boat!" Freddie said firmly.

"But I want to go home!" Flossie wailed.

"Oh, all right," Freddie said, a little annoyed

at his sister. He thought, "If I go home now, my little boat will be lost forever!"

Both children again paddled very hard with their hands, but the rowboat drifted farther and farther away from the shore. It was headed around a bend.

"Look, Freddie!" Flossie cried out. "An island. Let's land there!"

"Okay," Freddie agreed. "Maybe we can find someone to row us home and get my sailboat!"

The wind blew the boat nearer and nearer the

island. "Watch out! We're going to bump!" Flossie called.

At that moment the boat did bump on the shore of the island. Freddie stood up. "Come on, Flossie!" he said. "Let's explore!"

But as Flossie rose to take her brother's hand, a harsh voice called out:

"Get away from here! Don't land on this island!"

"Who's that?" Flossie whispered, her face white.

"I don't know, but we'd better leave!" her twin said, sitting down quickly.

They managed to turn the boat around so it was heading toward the shore of the lake.

But the wind was still blowing strongly up the lake, and the children could make no headway.

"Let's yell, Flossie!" Freddie said. "Maybe someone will hear and come for us."

"Help! Help!" the small twins shouted.

At this moment Nan, Bert, Harry, and Mrs. Smith were standing on the shore. Hal had brought up his canoe. There was no sign of the small twins.

"Freddie! Flossie!" Nan and Bert shouted.

"Listen!" Dorothy commanded. "I think I hear someone calling."

The five children became quiet. From far

down the lake they heard the cry: "Help!"

"That sounds like Freddie!" Nan said fearfully. "They must be in trouble!"

"Come on, Bert!" Hal called. "We'll take my canoe and go after them!"

The two boys jumped into the canoe and paddled swiftly out into the lake. In a short while the watchers on the bank saw two boats round the bend. Hal and Bert were paddling *The Swan,* with Freddie and Flossie seated in it. The borrowed rowboat was tied on behind.

"Thank goodness!" said Mrs. Smith in relief.

On the way back Hal picked up the lost oars, and Bert rescued the sailboat.

"We got scared by that awful voice," said Flossie.

"What voice?" Bert asked quickly.

The small twins told him. After they all reached the shore and the girls were making a fuss over Freddie and Flossie, Bert took the boys aside.

"I'd like to know who was on that island," he said. "How about our going over there tomorrow and looking around?"

"Sure! Let's go!" the other boys agreed.

As Bert and Harry walked back toward the group, Uncle William came hurrying from the Minturn boathouse. "Did any of you take out the *Firefly?*" he asked.

"No, sir," Bert replied, "we went in Hal's canoe. Why?"

"I thought the motor was sputtering a bit yesterday," Uncle William explained. "I planned to work on it before supper, but the boat's gone!"

"Gone!" Bert echoed in dismay. "We put it away last night. It must have been taken this morning!"

As soon as they reached home, he reported the loss to the police, who promised to look for the boat.

"Do you suppose Albert Garry stole our boat?" Dorothy wondered as she and the other two girls climbed into their beds that night.

"I don't know," Nan admitted sleepily. "But I wish we could catch him!"

The girls had been asleep only a short while when they were awakened by a loud ringing noise.

"What's that?" Nan cried, sitting up in bed.

CHAPTER XIII

THE STRANGER'S CAP

FLOSSIE and Dorothy also sat up. "It sounds like an alarm clock!" Dorothy said in bewilderment.

Nan turned on the light and peered at the clock on the bedside table. It was not an alarm clock. "Why, it's only eleven. Why would an alarm go off now?"

"I don't know," Dorothy replied, jumping out of bed, "but we'd better shut off the alarm."

"I'll get it," Flossie offered. "Where is the clock?"

Dorothy looked around the room. "I had an alarm clock, but I haven't used it in ages. I don't even remember where I put it."

"The ringing seems to be coming from your bookcase," Nan observed. She ran across the floor. The sound was indeed in that location, but there was no clock in sight.

118

Finally Flossie pulled an old battered clock from behind the books on the lowest shelf. "Here it is!" she said triumphantly.

Dorothy took the clock and pushed the little button which shut off the alarm bell. "That's funny," she said. "I don't remember putting the clock there, but I guess I must have."

"Well, I hope it doesn't go off again," Nan said as she turned out the light. "I'm sleepy!"

Everything was quiet and the girls were sound asleep when suddenly the room was again filled with the sound of ringing.

This time Dorothy sat up first. "Oh, no," she cried, "not again!"

Flossie slept on, but Nan jumped out of bed. She ran over to the bookshelves and picked up the alarm clock. "Why, this isn't ringing!" she exclaimed.

"There must be another clock!" Dorothy said with a yawn. "But where is it?"

The two girls ran around the room, peering under the beds, looking into bureau drawers and every other place they could think of. Still the ringing continued.

Finally Dorothy pulled open the door of the clothes closet. "It must be in here!" she called. She pushed the dresses aside and picked a clock from one of the pockets of the shoe bag on the door.

"Why did you put a clock in there?" Nan asked curiously.

Dorothy laughed. "I didn't, but I think I know who did!"

"Bert and Harry!" Nan exclaimed. "They're getting even with us for that bottle we put in the water!"

At this moment Flossie awakened. "What are you doing up?" she asked sleepily. "Is it morning?"

Nan and Dorothy told her about the second clock, and she laughed. But before anything else was said, Flossie was fast asleep again.

The next morning when the girls came down to breakfast Bert and Harry were already at the table. "Hi!" Bert said. "Did you girls sleep well last night?"

"Just fine!" Nan replied brightly.

"Of course, we did hear some bells ringing," Dorothy put in. "Did they bother you?"

"Never heard a thing," Bert declared innocently.

The boys grinned and went on with their breakfast. A few minutes later, Aunt Emily came in with the message that Mrs. Weller had called to invite all the children to lunch at the amusement park. She had some news for them.

"Do you suppose it's about Mr. Weller?" Nan asked excitedly.

"We'll have to put off our trip to the island," Bert said to Harry in a low tone. "I'll call Hal and tell him we can't make it."

When the six children arrived at the Lakeside Park, Cindy was waiting for them at the gate. She led them to an attractive outdoor restaurant where Mrs. Weller had reserved a large table.

"This is pretty!" Flossie said admiringly, as she looked around at the other tables covered with bright-colored cloths.

As the children enjoyed delicious sandwiches and chocolate milk, Mrs. Weller, a happy smile on her face, said:

"I've had a phone call from Mr. White at the airplane factory. He says one of their search planes has sighted a man on an island in the ocean near where my husband went down."

"I'm sure it's Daddy Pete!" Cindy's face shone.

Mrs. Weller went on, "The man had placed white stones to form the letters I and A on the ground in an open area."

"Are the search planes going to land on the island?" Bert asked excitedly.

Mrs. Weller explained that the island was very small and there appeared to be no place for a plane to land. "They're going to send a helicopter out from an airfield in the Azores, which is the nearest group of islands," she said.

"That's wonderful!" Nan said. "We're so happy for you!"

"If the man is my husband, you children will deserve the credit for his rescue," said Cindy's mother.

There was much excited chatter while her guests ate their ice cream and cake.

When it died down, Flossie said, "Do you think while we're here we could try to catch the fairy?"

"Yes, let's go there!" Bert agreed. "Harry hasn't seen the fairy castle."

Nan and Dorothy decided they would not make the visit. "Maybe we can help you in your booth," Nan suggested shyly to Cindy's mother.

"I'd be glad to have you girls," Mrs. Weller said gratefully. "We're sometimes very busy in the afternoons."

Bert and Harry and the small twins thanked their hostess, then went off in the direction of the Fairyland attraction. Nan and Dorothy walked over to the booth with Mrs. Weller and Cindy.

Mrs. Weller removed the "Closed" sign and raised the shutters. Then Nan and Dorothy helped her arrange her wares. They piled the sandals, scarves, and bags on the counter and hung the straw hats by strings from the edge of the canopy roof. They had just finished this when a boy of about ten came up to the booth.

"What would you like?" Nan asked. "We have some good puzzles."

The boy looked wistful but shook his head. "No," he said, "I've come for a cloth cap—one with a visor."

Mrs. Weller had heard him. "There are some back of you, Dorothy," she said.

Dorothy picked up the pile of caps and took them over to the boy. She rummaged through the collection and picked out one.

"This looks like a small one," she said. "Try it on."

"Oh, no, it's not for me," the boy said. "It's for a man."

"What size does he take?" Nan asked.

"I don't know. He just gave me this dollar and told me to come over here and buy a cap for him."

"Is he a big man?" Dorothy inquired, looking through the pile of caps again.

"No, he's sort of small and his hair sticks up on top of his head," the boy replied.

"This is a medium size," Dorothy drew out a cap. "And it's just a dollar. Maybe it would do."

"Thanks." The boy grabbed the cap, put a dollar bill on the counter, and ran off.

Nan looked at Dorothy in excitement. "He said the man was small and had hair that stuck up! Do you think he could possibly be Albert Garry?"

"I never thought of that," Dorothy cried. "Let's follow that boy!"

With a hurried word to Mrs. Weller, the two girls left the booth. When they caught up to the boy, they found him standing by a drinking fountain. He looked puzzled.

"Did the cap fit?" Dorothy asked as they walked up to him.

"I don't know," the boy replied. "The man told me to bring it here to him, but he's gone!"

"That's too bad," Nan said sympathetically. "But perhaps he'll be back."

They left the boy standing uncertainly by the fountain and returned to the booth. "If it was Garry, we've missed him again," Nan remarked with a sigh.

In the meantime Bert, Harry, and the small twins had made their way toward Fairyland.

Flossie skipped along beside Bert. "Perhaps if we took the fairy some candy she'd let us catch her," Flossie said with a little grin.

"Or maybe the Bobbseys' little fat fairy wants some!" Bert teased her.

"Look, Bert!" Freddie called. "There are some candy apples!" He pointed to a stand where a man was selling bright red apples mounted on sticks.

"I'll treat you!" Harry suggested, pulling some coins from his pocket.

Freddie and Flossie each picked up one of the sticks. The large apples had been coated with a thick layer of hardened syrup.

"Ooh, it's heavy!" Flossie said as she lifted the sweet to her mouth.

"Let's have a duel, Flossie!" Freddie cried. He held out the stick with the apple on it and lunged toward his twin.

But as he did so, the stick broke and the apple landed *plop* on Flossie's toe!

"Ow!" she cried. "That hurt, Freddie!"

"I'm sorry," Freddie apologized. "And I lost my apple!"

"If you'll promise to eat it and not throw it around, I'll buy you another," Bert said.

Freddie said he would be careful, so in a minute the small twins were hurrying toward the fairy castle, trying to finish the apples before they went in to see the fairy.

When they reached the little castle, Flossie pointed out the sign to Harry. "We saw the fairy the other time we were here," she explained, "but when we tried to catch her she went behind a curtain and disappeared!"

"Bert and I'll get her this time!" Harry said with a grin.

"Sure," Bert agreed. "We should be smart enough to figure out what happens!"

As had occurred before, when the children pushed open the little front door, a bell tinkled its welcome.

"The fairy's in here!" Flossie whispered as she tiptoed toward the wide door leading from the entrance hall.

The children entered the room, then stopped. The brown curtain hung in front of the fireplace.

"Something's behind there!" Freddie declared. He ran across the room and jerked the curtain aside. As he did this the children saw two tiny silver slippers disappearing up the chimney.

A voice drifted back to them. "Catch me if you can!"

CHAPTER XIV

A CHIMNEY HUNT

AS THE voice of the fairy died away, Bert dashed to the fireplace. He bent over and peered up the chimney.

"That's funny!" he exclaimed. "Steps go up inside. There weren't any the other time. I remember looking for them!"

"Hurry, Bert!" Freddie exclaimed impatiently. "Let's follow the fairy!"

The stairs were narrow and very steep. Bert made his way first, then Flossie, followed by Freddie, and Harry at the end.

"Ooh! It's dark!" Flossie said as she pulled herself up after Bert.

"I think we're coming to the end," Bert called to the others. The next minute he pushed open a door and stepped out onto a little balcony. The others followed.

128

"But the fairy's not here!" Flossie cried, looking all around.

"Here are some more stairs," Freddie announced. He had been walking around the balcony and had seen steps which led down to the ground in back of the castle.

Quickly the four children ran down the stairs and around the little castle. But there was still no sign of the fairy.

"Maybe the chimney stairs go up farther," Bert finally suggested. "The fairy may be on the roof."

Freddie led the way this time. They climbed back up to the balcony.

"The steps don't go any farther," he reported. "The fairy *must* have gone out to the balcony."

"But where is she now?" Flossie wailed, as they stepped outside.

"She probably went into the house," Harry said. "Let's look around there."

"I think she's one of Santa Claus's fairies," Flossie said suddenly.

"Why, Flossie?" Freddie asked.

"Because she went up the chimney," Flossie stated with an impish grin.

The others laughed and agreed.

"Maybe she went down the chimney again while we were looking around on the ground," Harry suggested.

"Then we should go down, too," Bert said. He went into the chimney and started the descent, followed by the others.

When they reached the bottom of the steps Freddie and Flossie ran out into the entrance hall. There stood the fairy!

Now the children could see that she was a very small young lady. She had wavy golden hair, shining blue eyes, and a happy smile. She wore a ballet costume and wings and carried a wand with a star on top.

"Come!" She beckoned to the twins. "You have found me! Tell me your wishes and I will see if they can be granted."

"I'd like a new fire engine!" Freddie said at once.

"And I want a new doll," Flossie declared.

The fairy smiled. "I'm sure your wishes will be granted at Christmas," she said, "if you are good children.

"And now," she continued, "since you caught me in my castle, you are members of Fairyland! Here are your rewards!"

The fairy went to a table in the hall and returned with two little packages. "Open them!" she said with a smile.

Eagerly Freddie and Flossie untied the gold cord and opened the boxes. In Flossie's was a

There stood the fairy!

little wand with a tinsel star at the top! Freddie received a tiny silver horn.

"Thank you!" the small twins chorused, their blue eyes shining with delight.

Bert and Harry had been looking on with interest. Now Bert spoke up. "Could you tell us how you vanished the other day? I didn't see any stairway then."

"You may call me Hada," the young woman said. "That is the Spanish word for fairy. Yes, I will tell you my secret. There is a little button at the top of the stairs. When I push it, the steps fold up flat against the side of the chimney and are not noticed. The castle has many doors. So I run down the stairs from the balcony and slip back indoors without being seen."

"So that's what happened the first time we were here!" Bert exclaimed.

"That's right!" Hada laughed. "It wouldn't be so much fun if you caught the fairy the first time you tried, now would it?"

Freddie and Flossie shook their heads in agreement.

"Do you always tell children their wishes will come true?" Harry asked curiously.

Hada said this was only when children wished for something which would be good for them, and she thought it was possible for the parents to see that the wishes were granted.

The four children said good-by to Hada and hurried over to Mrs. Weller's booth to tell the girls of their adventure. Nan and Dorothy, in turn, told of their suspicion that Garry was in the park.

"We think he sent that boy to buy him a cap to replace the one he lost when he stole Hal's canoe," Nan said.

"Did you tell all this to the police?" Bert asked.

"Not yet," Nan replied. "Do you want to come with us?"

Bert, Nan, and Dorothy found Officer Weaver at the entrance to the Underground City. When Nan and Dorothy told their story, the policeman pushed his hat to the back of his head and mopped his forehead.

"I don't see how Garry could be in the park," he said. "We've been watching this place pretty carefully all during the past week. But thanks anyhow for telling me."

As the children left the park a short time later, Dorothy remarked, "We'll have time for a swim before supper if you want. It's just between high and low tides now, and the water will be nice."

"Good!" Bert exclaimed. "I'd like to get in a little practice on my crawl."

Freddie and Flossie decided just to go wading.

The four older children dashed upstairs when they reached the Minturns' house and a few minutes later met on the porch ready for a swim.

"The water looks great!" Bert said as they ran down to the beach.

The ocean was covered with large swells which broke into whitecaps as they neared the shore. The children dashed into the water and dived under the waves.

When they came up, shaking the water from their eyes, Dorothy said, "How about giving Nan and me a chance to duck fight?"

"Sure!" Bert agreed. "Climb on!" He hoisted Dorothy to his shoulders while Harry did the same to Nan. Then the boys stood close together, facing each other.

This time, instead of merely splashing water, Nan and Dorothy decided to try to unseat each other. They pushed and pulled, each one trying to make the other fall from her perch.

Between the undertow which had begun to swirl about their legs and the struggles of the girls, Bert and Harry had difficulty keeping their footing. Suddenly Nan landed a lucky push and Dorothy slid off Bert's shoulders! She came up spouting water and laughing.

"Okay," she said, "I guess you won this time, but watch out!"

Nan, Dorothy, and Harry waded ashore and sat on the sand to rest, but Bert stayed out in the water. He swam with strong, even strokes in a course parallel to the beach. Then he turned and swam back.

When at last he came out and dropped down beside the others, the lifeguard strolled over. "I've been watching you, Bert," he said. "You're going great guns with that crawl!"

Bert reddened with pleasure. "Thanks," he said. "I've been working hard on it."

"Well, keep it up!" the young man said cheerfully. He scanned the shoreline and saw no one in the water. "It's time for me to go off duty now. Guess I'll go change into my clothes. Be seeing you!" He walked up the beach and disappeared into the beachhouse.

Dorothy stood up. "I'm starved," she said. "It must be about time for supper."

But before the children could start back, a cry reached their ears.

"What's that?" asked Nan.

"I think it came from the water," Dorothy said. She peered out over the ocean.

"Look!" Harry cried, pointing. "There's a man's head bobbing out there!"

"Help!" came the cry again. "Help!"

"He's in trouble!" Bert shouted and started to run.

He reached the water and plunged into the surf. Bert swam strongly toward the spot where the head had been seen.

The other five raced to the edge of the water. "I'll help Bert!" Harry said. "You girls and Freddie stay here!"

But Dorothy, who had become an excellent swimmer since she lived by the ocean, had already started after Bert. Although Nan was a good swimmer, she knew she was not strong enough to help now. She turned and dashed down the beach to summon the lifeguard.

Freddie and Flossie watched anxiously from the water's edge.

By this time Harry and Dorothy had reached Bert. They saw the Bobbsey boy's head appear above the water.

"I have him!" Bert said. Then he gasped, "Help me! He's—"

CHAPTER XV

ISLAND HIDE-OUT

BERT disappeared under the water. The swimmer in distress had become panicky and grabbed the boy around the neck. There was a brief struggle, then Bert rose to the surface again, holding the man.

"I had to hit him to make him let go," Bert panted. "But he's all right."

The man shook his head and looked around. "I'm okay now."

"Just rest your hands on my shoulder," Bert directed, "and I'll tow you to shore."

The man did as he was told. Dorothy and Harry swam alongside Bert, ready to help if needed. When the four staggered onto the beach, the lifeguard, Nan, and the small twins ran up.

"Are you all right, Mr. Cole?" the guard asked. "What happened?"

"I'm okay," the man said. "I got a cramp out there and couldn't swim. This boy saved my life!"

The lifeguard turned to Bert and put out his hand. "You did a wonderful job! I didn't know Mr. Cole was out there or I never would have left the beach!"

"Well, everything's turned out all right," Mr. Cole said, "thanks to this young man here!"

Bert reddened at the praise. "I'm glad we heard you call," he said modestly.

After a few more words of thanks, Mr. Cole went off with the lifeguard, who had offered to drive him home. The six children climbed the path to the Minturns' house.

"You really were brave, Bert!" Flossie said admiringly, and the others agreed heartily.

Bert grinned. "I just happened to get there first! Dorothy and Harry would have saved him if I hadn't!"

But at the supper table when the grownups heard the story, they all declared that Bert had been a real hero. To change the subject, Bert asked if there were any report about the stolen boat.

"I've just called the police," Uncle William spoke up. "They haven't found it yet."

"Maybe someone along the lakeshore has seen

it," Bert suggested. "Do you mind if we ask?"

"It's a good idea."

The older children went over to the lake. They walked along the shore road, stopping at each cottage to ask about the missing motorboat. No one remembered having seen it since Sunday evening after the water carnival.

"It must have been taken during the night," Dorothy decided, "or someone would have noticed it. We may as well give up for tonight."

The next morning Bert thought of his resolve to explore the island where Freddie and Flossie had heard the threatening voice. When he mentioned it to Dorothy, she had a suggestion.

"Let's all go there and have a picnic!" she said. "Maybe Hal will take us in his canoe."

Bert ran to the telephone and called Hal. When he heard the plan Hal agreed at once. "I don't think my canoe will hold us all. But I can get that rowboat Freddie and Flossie borrowed the other day. I'll meet you at the boathouse at eleven."

Dorothy took the telephone from Bert. "We'll bring the picnic," she said. "Is there anything you especially like?"

"I could go for some chocolate cake!" Hal replied with a laugh.

"You'll have it!" Dorothy promised.

Dinah chuckled when Dorothy told her about Hal's request. "I'll make the biggest, most chocolatey cake you ever saw!" she said, hurrying to get out the ingredients.

By eleven o'clock the lunch was packed in a straw basket. "Now you watch this cake!" Dinah warned, as she handed Nan a big pasteboard box tied with string.

Hal was waiting at the boathouse when the Bobbseys and Dorothy arrived. The canoe and the rowboat were drawn up on the bank, side by side.

"We have a choc'late cake with marshmallow frosting!" Flossie said with a giggle.

"Wow!" Hal exclaimed. "That sounds great!"

It was decided that Bert, Nan, and Flossie would go in Hal's canoe, while Dorothy and Harry would take Freddie in the borrowed craft. Bert got in first and went forward to the bow paddle. Then Hal helped Nan and Flossie in. They settled themselves on cushions in the bottom. Nan held the cake box.

The lunch basket was put in the rowboat with Freddie. Hal and Harry pushed the two craft out into the water and jumped in. Soon they were gliding along quietly side by side.

"It's fun to have a lake picnic even if we don't find anyone on the island!" Dorothy called.

Presently the boats rounded the bend in the shoreline and the island lay before them. In another few minutes they touched shore. Bert jumped out and held Hal's canoe steady.

"Hold this, Flossie, while I get out," Nan directed, handing the cake box to Flossie, who stood behind her.

Nan stepped ashore and turned to take the cake from Flossie. At that moment the canoe tipped. Flossie tried desperately to keep her balance. As she teetered back and forth the pasteboard box slipped from her grasp!

"Look out!" Hal shouted. "The cake!"

Nan made a quick lunge forward. With one hand she caught the string on the box!

"Good catch!" Hal and Bert cried at the same time. Then Hal shook his head in mock despair. "I thought my cake was going to the fishes for sure!" he said with a grin.

By this time Harry and Dorothy had beached their rowboat. Freddie ran up with the picnic basket.

"Shall we eat first or explore?" Nan asked.

"Let's eat!" Freddie spoke up. "I'm hungry!"

"Okay!" Dorothy rumpled her little cousin's hair. "We don't want anyone dying of starvation!"

"This looks like a good place here," Hal observed, indicating the clean, white beach.

The island was thickly wooded, but on three sides it was bordered by white sand. Nan and Dorothy, with Flossie's help, quickly spread out the picnic cloth and set out paper plates and napkins. Bert opened the soft drinks and poured them into paper cups.

"Dinah gave us a good picnic!" Dorothy said as they began to eat the chicken and ham sandwiches and the potato salad.

"I'm saving room for the cake!" Hal announced as he turned down a third sandwich.

"Ooh, isn't it bee-yoo-ti-ful!" Flossie exclaimed when the lid of the cake box was lifted. The big round cake was covered with a snowy white frosting from which bumps of marshmallow rose in little mounds.

Each of the children had two pieces. Freddie considered having a third. "You'd better not!" Flossie giggled. "You'll be so heavy you'll sink the boat!"

At that moment Bert gave a yell and held up his arm. A giant crab was clinging to his wrist! The boy jerked his arm as hard as he could. The crab flew off and landed some distance away.

"Oh, Bert, did it nip you?" Nan asked anxiously as she ran to her brother.

Bert examined his wrist. "I guess it didn't bite me," he admitted, "but it sure did pinch!"

As Dorothy started to walk over the crab, Harry yelled, "Look out!"

Dorothy bent over and picked it up. "Don't worry," she said. "He's harmless!" With a quick movement she tossed it to Bert.

The boy jumped aside and stared down at the crab. Then he looked sheepish. "The crab is made of rubber!" Bert exclaimed. "Okay, Dorothy!" he said with a grin. "I guess this makes us even for the alarm clocks!"

Still laughing about the rubber crab, the children gathered up the remains of their picnic.

When everything was tidy again Bert said eagerly, "Shall we explore the island now? I'd like to find out who scared Freddie and Flossie the other day."

"Just a minute," Hal replied. "I want to make sure the boats are safe." He ran over and pulled the craft up farther on the beach. "I'd hate to be marooned here!"

"Does anyone live on this island, Dorothy?" Nan asked as the children walked into the woods.

"I don't think so. People come here for picnics," Dorothy replied, "but I never heard that anybody lives here."

The woods seemed very quiet. Even the birds were still. Then a queer little honking sound broke the silence.

"What's that?" Flossie asked in surprise.

Dorothy put her finger to her lips and tiptoed over to a little bush. "There!" She pointed. "Tree frogs."

Clinging to a branch of the bush were two grayish-brown frogs not more than two inches long. Their throats were puffed out into round yellow sacs.

"They're blowing up!" Flossie whispered.

"They do that when they're talking to each other," Dorothy explained.

Freddie had joined his twin. "Let's take the

frogs home," he suggested. He put out his hand to pick up a frog, but the little animals hopped farther up on the branch and disappeared behind the leaves.

"Come on, Freddie and Flossie!" Bert called. "Stay with us so you won't get lost."

The children went on into the woods, looking carefully for a sign that anyone had been there before them. They came to a little brook, and all of them took off their sneakers to wade across it.

As Bert sat down on the ground to put his shoes on again, he glanced up the bank of the stream. "Say!" he called. "That looks like some sort of a shelter!"

The others followed him to a crude lean-to. Several branches had been placed across the space between two trees, the ends resting in the notches where the limbs met the tree trunk. Leafy branches had been laid over these to form a roof.

"And look!" Nan pointed out. "Someone had a campfire here!"

Hal bent down and felt the bits of burned wood and ash. "They're still warm!" he said. "Whoever built this fire hasn't been gone long!"

"Which way do you suppose he went?" Harry asked eagerly.

"I suggest we fan out and search," Bert said.

"Nan, you and Hal go to the left; Harry and Dorothy go to the right and I'll go straight ahead with Freddie and Flossie. The first person who sees anyone, call out and the rest of us will come!"

They did as Bert suggested and once more the search went forward. But they had no success. After a half hour the three groups met back on the beach.

"It's no use," Bert said in a discouraged tone. "Whoever was here must have left before we arrived."

Dorothy had been peering at the sky. "I think we'd better start home," she said in a worried tone. "It looks as if a storm is coming up and this lake gets horribly rough."

Quickly the children put the picnic basket in Hal's canoe and took their places. Just as Harry shoved off in the borrowed rowboat a brilliant streak of lightning flashed across the sky. Nan, who was seated in the canoe, suddenly called out:

"Look! There's a man in an outboard motorboat! Is it the *Firefly,* Dorothy?"

CHAPTER XVI

BOAT ADRIFT!

"MOTORBOAT!" Dorothy echoed.

"Just leaving that far stretch of beach," Nan replied. "We didn't see any boat there before. The man in it must have had it hidden under some overhanging trees."

Dorothy gazed at the boat intently. "It looks like our *Firefly*," she said, "but I can't see it too well so far away."

"Well, we sure can't catch it in a canoe!" Hal said.

The children watched as the motorboat sped toward the other side of the island and disappeared.

"We can report it to the police," Dorothy said. "Let's have a race to shore!" She dug her oars into the water and sent the borrowed boat leaping forward.

"Okay!" Bert and Hal called, and they, too, began to paddle furiously.

The wind had come up and the lake water was very choppy. It took all the children's strength to make any headway against the waves. Water kept splashing into both boats.

"I hope we can get home before the rain starts!" Dorothy called over. "I wouldn't like to be out on this lake in a bad storm. It's shallow here, and you ought to see how rough it gets in a high wind!"

The trip home seemed much longer than the one on the way to the island. But at last the children ran their craft up to the Bingham boathouse.

"I'll put them inside," Hal said. "You kids run on before it rains."

Bert and Harry stayed to help, however, while Nan, Dorothy, and the small twins hurried to the Minturn house. Just as they reached the porch the rain poured down in torrents.

Mrs. Bobbsey opened the door. "I'm so glad you're home," she said. "I was afraid you'd be caught in the storm!"

Nan told her mother that Bert and Harry would be along as soon as the boats were locked in the boathouse. She mentioned having seen a motorboat that might be the Minturns'.

"I'll call the police," Dorothy's mother said.

Freddie went out to the kitchen for a cookie. Dinah looked worried. "Did you see Snoop anywhere?" she asked. "I've looked all over the house, and I can't find him!"

"Oh!" Freddie cried. "Snoop's afraid of storms! I hope he's not outside."

Freddie reported Snoop's disappearance to the others. Bert and Harry had reached home by this time, and all the children searched through the house for the cat. They peered under beds and in closets. But Snoop was not around.

"I'm going to look outside," Freddie said determinedly.

"Let's all go," Nan suggested. "It'll be fun in the rain!"

So the six children put on slickers, rain hats, and boots and ran out into the storm. They searched under all the bushes without finding Snoop. Then Freddie went into the garage.

"Here, Snoop," he called as he peered about.

A faint meow answered him. Stooping down, Freddie looked under Uncle William's car. There, huddled up in a little black ball, was Snoop!

"Come on out, Snoopy," Freddie coaxed. But the cat refused to budge.

"I guess I'll have to get him," Freddie said to himself. The little boy flattened himself on the floor of the garage and wriggled under the car. He reached out, managed to grasp Snoop in one hand, and inched his way back.

"I'm glad you found him," Flossie said happily when Freddie carried Snoop to the porch.

"Put him in the house," Nan suggested. "We're all going to stay out here and watch the storm."

By this time the ocean was a mass of whitecaps. The waves crashed on the shore, and the rain came in great gusts.

"Ooh, isn't it 'citing?" Flossie said, her blue eyes sparkling.

At this minute Hal ran onto the porch. "Hey," he called, "there's an outboard motorboat in trouble on the lake! The water's very rough, and the man in the boat doesn't seem to be able to make any headway!"

"We'd better call the police," Dorothy said, starting for the door. "They have a rescue launch."

The officer in charge assured Dorothy that help would be sent at once.

"Let's go up to the police boathouse," she suggested when she hung up the telephone. "It's not far."

When Nan went in the house to tell her mother where they were going, Mrs. Bobbsey told the small twins to stay at home. "I'm afraid you would blow away," she said with a smile.

Freddie and Flossie were disappointed, but Aunt Emily brought out a new jigsaw puzzle and they were soon lost in the problem of trying to put it together.

In the meantime the older children ran down to the lake shore. "I don't see a boat," Harry remarked as they reached the water.

"Sure, there it is!" Hal pointed out over the gray lake.

By straining their eyes the children could see a small boat tossing up and down on the choppy water. It seemed to be completely out of control.

"Oh, it'll be swamped!" Dorothy cried out fearfully. "Let's see if the police have started yet!"

She led the way along the shore until they came to the headquarters of the police lake patrol. As the five children ran up, two officers dressed in oilskins were just boarding a trim launch.

"We're going right out!" one of the men said, recognizing Dorothy. "Thanks for calling us. Anyone on that lake in this storm is really in trouble!"

"Would you take us along?" Bert asked hopefully.

"I'm afraid not, son," the policeman replied. "It may be pretty dangerous."

"We'll be careful, and I bet we could even help you," Hal spoke up.

The officer looked at the tall boy. "Well, we *are* shorthanded," he said. "Maybe you fellows *can* help us. The girls may come along if they'll stay in the wheelhouse with the pilot, Bill Cooper. I'm Fred Palmer."

"Thank you!" Nan said gratefully. "We'll try not to get in your way."

Bill Cooper took his place at the wheel of the launch while Fred Palmer walked to the stern where there was a post with a rope around it.

Dorothy climbed aboard the boat and followed the policeman into the wheelhouse. She sat down on the narrow bench which was built in the space under the window.

Nan came next. As she stepped on the wet deck, her feet slipped from under her. Across the wood planks she skidded, straight for the open railing!

Quickly Bert dashed forward. He grabbed the back of Nan's raincoat and stopped her slide. "Whew! You were just in time, Bert," Nan exclaimed as she scrambled to her feet. "I was sure I was going over the side!"

She made her way forward to join Dorothy while Bert, Harry, and Hal clung to the railing near the stern. The launch sped through the choppy water.

It was still raining heavily, and the visibility was bad. The policeman at the wheel peered into the distance. The little motorboat was still bobbing on the waves.

"I don't see how he has managed to keep afloat!" Cooper muttered. "These waves are certainly big enough to turn over a boat of that size!"

As the police launch drew nearer the helpless

boat, Dorothy stood up and looked through the window. "Why, that looks like our stolen boat! It is! It's the *Firefly!*" she exclaimed in astonishment.

In another minute the patrolman cut the launch's motor. The man in the stern picked up a megaphone and called out to the man in the drifting boat, "Are you all right?"

The occupant, who had been huddled in the bottom, sat up slowly. He cupped his hands and shouted back, "Yes. But my motor's conked out!"

The pilot of the launch came as close to the motorboat as he could without upsetting it. "I'll throw you a tow!" Fred Palmer called to the helpless man.

He unwound the rope from the post and tossed it toward the stranded boat. *Plop!* It fell short as the *Firefly* drifted farther away.

Fred hauled in the rope and tried again. This time it reached its goal.

The man grabbed the rope and tied it around one of the seats. Then a particularly high wave struck, tilting the boat at a dangerous angle. The man teetered, crying out that he could not swim, and tried to regain his balance. The next moment he tumbled over the side!

"I'll get him!" Bert offered. He stripped off his slicker and boots and dived into the lake.

"I'd better help!" Fred said.

By the time he hit the water Bert had reached the stranger. The patrolman swam over to them and, between the two, they got the panicky man to the launch. Harry and Hal leaned over and pulled him up. Bert and Fred tied the disabled motorboat to the stern of the launch, then climbed back onto the launch. The rescued man sank to the deck, exhausted.

Nan and Dorothy ran out of the wheelhouse with blankets which they put around Bert and the two men. After a few words from Patrolman Palmer, Hal hurried to the wheelhouse and returned with a thermos of hot tea.

"Here, drink this," he said, pouring some into a paper cup and offering it to the rescued man.

The stranger sat up and took the tea. He was thin and blond and, though his hair was wet, one lock stood up on the crown of his head.

Bert looked at him closely. Then he asked, "Aren't you Albert Garry?"

CHAPTER XVII

GOOD NEWS!

ON HEARING Bert's question, the stranger acted startled. Then he closed his eyes and weakly shook his head.

"I guess he's about all in," Officer Palmer remarked. "We'll take him into the wheelhouse. At least he'll be dry there."

When the shivering man had been seated in the pilothouse, the policeman came back on deck where the children were standing. The rain had since stopped.

"Do you know who this man is?" the officer asked Bert.

"I think he's Albert Garry," Bert replied and told Palmer of the children's efforts to catch the man who had stolen the large sum of money from the airline.

The patrolman whistled in surprise. "If this boat thief *is* Albert Garry," he said, "we're in luck. The Ocean Cliff police have been looking day and night for him!"

"Even if he isn't Garry," Dorothy spoke up, "he had our stolen boat!"

"That's right!" Palmer agreed. "We'll take him to headquarters and question him."

The police launch was nearing the dock and in another moment pulled alongside it. Palmer grabbed a line to throw over the mooring post.

As the rope coiled around the anchor, the suspect suddenly raced from the wheelhouse and vaulted over the railing onto the dock. "Catch him!" Bill Cooper shouted.

Quick as a flash Bert and Hal ran after the

fleeing man. Palmer stopped only long enough to make the line fast, then joined in the chase.

When the fugitive reached the end of the dock he hesitated a moment, as if trying to decide which way to run. Bert made a flying tackle and grabbed the man's feet. With a crash, the stranger fell to the ground.

"Good work, fellows!" Palmer cried as he pounded up. He jerked the man to his feet and snapped handcuffs on him.

"You have some explaining to do," he said. "We'll take you to headquarters and give you a chance to talk there!"

The policemen thanked the children for their help and herded the prisoner toward a waiting patrol car.

"Do you suppose he *is* Albert Garry?" Nan asked excitedly. "Won't it be wonderful if we've really caught him?"

"At least we have the *Firefly* back!" Dorothy reminded them. "And there's nothing the matter with it except the boat's out of gas!"

The boys carried over a can and poured in the fuel. The children went to the boathouse, then Hal said good-by. "Some excitement!" he added, grinning.

The others hurried to the house to tell Freddie and Flossie and the grownups of their adventure on the lake.

Dinah listened with amazement to the story. When it came to the rescue of the man in the drifting boat, she threw up her hands. "That Bert!" she exclaimed. "He's saved two men in two days! I'm right proud of him!"

Bert laughed. "I didn't exactly save them by myself," he reminded the cook.

"I think all you children have done a good job on your puzzling cases at the seashore," Mr. Bobbsey spoke up. "And I hope the criminal has been found."

The next morning Bert called police headquarters. "That man you caught yesterday," Officer Weaver told him, "refuses to say anything. But an official from Allied Cargo Airlines is on his way here to try to identify him. If he does turn out to be Garry, I'll call to let you know!"

"Thanks, Officer Weaver," Bert said. "We'll be waiting to hear from you!"

The children stayed within earshot of the telephone, but it was almost noon before it rang. Bert dashed to answer. "The man's Albert Garry, all right," Officer Weaver said. "The airline official identified him positively. But the fellow still won't talk, and we don't know where he has hidden the money!"

"I'm glad you caught the bad man," Flossie said when Bert told the others the news.

"Yes," sighed Nan, "but I wish we could find the money, too!"

"Maybe he hid it on the island," Harry suggested.

"Could be. We might go over there again and look around," Dorothy said.

"Remember, Cindy said she saw that man," Flossie reminded the others. "And he had a paper shopping bag."

"With the money in it!" Freddie exclaimed.

"But we don't know the money was in the bag," Nan objected. "He could have hidden it anywhere!"

"Why would he be running around with a paper shopping bag unless he had the stolen money in it?" Bert said thoughtfully. "I vote we go back to the amusement park and look for the bag!"

After a little discussion the children decided to go to Lakeside that afternoon. When Nan told her mother their plan, Mrs. Bobbsey smiled. "Go ahead," she said. "I know you'll never be happy until you've solved this puzzle!"

The six children started out after lunch. "Let's go see Cindy first," Flossie said as they went through the entrance gate.

When the group reached Mrs. Weller's booth they found it closed. "I wonder where Cindy is?" Flossie said in disappointment.

Just then, Nan caught sight of the little girl and her mother coming from the outdoor restaurant. Their faces were beaming.

Cindy ran up to the visitors. "Oh, the most wonderful thing has happened!" she bubbled.

"Your father has been found?" Nan cried.

Cindy nodded, her brown eyes shining with happiness. "You tell them about it, Mother," she urged.

Mrs. Weller told the children that she had just received another telephone call from Mr. White, of the airplane factory. "He told me that the helicopter from the Azores was able to rescue the man from the small island. And he is Captain Weller!"

"How marvelous!" Nan cried. "When will he be home?"

Cindy's mother explained that Captain Weller had been taken to a hospital at the airfield in the Azores. "He is very weak from his ordeal," she said, "but they expect him to be ready to fly home next week!"

Flossie threw her arms around Cindy. "Oh, aren't you 'cited?" she cried. "I hope we can meet your daddy!"

"Yes," Mrs. Weller said. "I know Captain Weller will want to meet the children who are responsible for his rescue!"

The visitors were so interested in the news of

Captain Weller that they had almost forgotten why they had come to the amusement park. It was Nan who suddenly remembered.

"Cindy," she said, "the first day we were here you told us you had seen a thin, blond man carrying a big paper shopping bag."

"Yes, I did."

"We think he may be the man who stole a lot of money from an airplane," Nan went on. "Can you tell us exactly where you saw him and where he went?"

Cindy thought a moment. Then she said, "I was standing here by Mother's booth when he ran by. I looked at him because he was running and because he had that big bag."

"Then where did he go?" Bert asked.

"He ran down there toward the Underground City," Cindy replied. "I didn't really see where he stopped."

"I think he hid the money in the Underground City," Freddie said. "I know I saw the man in there," he insisted.

Bert reminded his little brother that the police had made a thorough search of the Underground City without finding anything.

"Then maybe the money is hidden outside the City," Flossie suggested.

"That could be it!" Bert exclaimed. "Let's give it a try!"

Cindy was as excited as the other children. "May I help them look, Mother?" she asked.

When she received permission, the group of children ran to the Underground City. The ride was doing a brisk business, with the little boats leaving the entrance every few minutes.

The low, green wooden building which housed the Underground City was surrounded by shrubbery. The children split into two groups with Nan, Dorothy, Harry, and Flossie going around one side while Bert, Freddie, and Cindy went the other way. Carefully, they looked under all the bushes. But when they met in front again no one had found the shopping bag.

Suddenly Cindy had a thought. "There's a little hollow back of the City," she said. "Maybe the thief went down there."

"We'll try that!" Bert cried, and they all ran to the rear of the building. There the land dropped sharply away into a small ravine. It was filled with low bushes.

Freddie and Flossie were the first to scramble down the incline, followed by the others. A few minutes passed while everyone pushed aside the overgrown shrubbery. Suddenly Flossie gave a squeal. "Here's something!" she cried.

From far under a thick bush she pulled a white paper bag. It was covered with blue stars!

CHAPTER XVIII

HAPPY REUNION

"OH BOY! Flossie, I think you've found the stolen money!" Bert exclaimed, taking the bag from his little sister.

While the other children watched breathlessly, Bert put his hand in the bag and pulled out a neat pile of hundred-dollar bills! They were held together by a paper band.

"Wow! There must be a fortune here!" Harry cried as Bert brought out package after package of the bills.

"We'd better call the police!" Nan reminded him.

Hurriedly Bert stuffed the money back into the bag, and the children made their way up to the Underground City. From there they ran to Mrs. Weller's booth.

Bert told her of their exciting find, then said,

"May we leave the money here while I call the police?"

"We'll guard it," Freddie volunteered, and Mrs. Weller smilingly agreed.

Nan went with Bert to make the telephone call from the restaurant. "Good work!" Officer Weaver exclaimed when Bert told him about finding the stolen money. "We'll be out there right away to pick it up!"

It was not long before a closed patrol car made its way through the park grounds and drew up at Mrs. Weller's booth. Passersby gaped as the officer jumped out and walked to the counter.

Proudly, Freddie handed over the dilapidated shopping bag. "Would you children like to come down to headquarters with me?" the kindly policeman asked as he tossed the money into the truck.

"Oh, yes!" they chorused.

"Okay," he said. "Bert, you and Nan ride up in front with me. The others can get in back with Fred Palmer."

Their friend of the lake patrol smiled a welcome. "I see you're following right through on this case!" he teased. "We'll have to make you regular members of the force!"

"We're detectives!" Flossie giggled.

In a short while the patrol car drew up in front of the Ocean Cliff Police Headquarters. "Maybe our friend Garry will talk a little when he sees this bag of groceries!" Officer Weaver said with a grin, putting the money on the chief's desk.

After he had met the Bobbsey twins and Dorothy and Harry, the chief ordered Albert Garry to be brought in. The prisoner stared sullenly at the children as he shuffled into the room. When he saw the white shopping bag on the chief's desk, he turned pale.

"Does this look familiar to you, Garry?" the chief asked sternly. "These children found it in Lakeside Amusement Park, and they tell me you were seen carrying it the day the money was stolen from the airline."

"Okay, so I took the money while we were unloading the plane," Garry said in a surly tone. "When the cops got on my trail and followed me to Lakeside, I hid it."

"I saw you in the Underground City!" Freddie piped up.

"Yes." The man glared at Freddie. "I would have been able to get away if that mob of cops hadn't swarmed over the park. I suppose you kids started that!"

"No. But the Bobbseys and their friends have been a great help to us," the police chief said.

"You may as well tell us how you managed to get away from us," Officer Weaver added. "Where had you been hiding before we picked you up yesterday?"

The thief admitted that he had stolen Hal's canoe from the lagoon while the boys were on shore registering for the water carnival. "The cops were watching all the exits, but they didn't think I could leave by water!" he sneered.

"Go on!" the police chief directed.

"Well, I beached the canoe, thinking I could hop a bus and come back later for the money when the excitement had died down."

"But you didn't do that," Nan spoke up. "You stayed around Ocean Cliff."

"That's right. I got to thinking I could hide out on the island. So I took a motorboat and set up a little camp."

"You're the one who yelled at us from the island, the day we lost our toy sailboat!" Flossie said accusingly.

Garry looked disgusted as he nodded. "These kids were always around upsetting my plans!" He pointed a grimy finger at Nan and Dorothy. "The next day when I went back to the park to get the money, I saw those two girls follow the boy I sent to buy me a cap.

"I decided to sit it out on the island and then a whole bunch of kids had a picnic there!" Garry shook his head in despair. "I got away in the boat and the motor conked out! I sure had bad luck all around!"

"But it was these same children who reported you in trouble on the lake. If they hadn't done that, you would have drowned!" Officer Weaver reminded him.

"Yeah, I guess I owe them that!" Garry said grudgingly.

The chief motioned to have the prisoner returned to his cell, and the man was taken away.

"The Ocean Cliff police have a lot to thank you children for," the chief said as he stood up to shake hands with the Bobbseys and Dorothy. "Without your sharp eyes and quick thinking that thief might not have been captured. I want you to meet Mr. Evans, president of Allied Cargo Airlines, and tell him how you solved his case."

The children were eager to tell their parents about the exciting events of the afternoon. That night at the supper table the full story of Garry and the hidden money was told.

Mr. Bobbsey said, "I'm glad you solved all your mysteries, because it's time for us to go home to Lakeport. The summer is almost over."

"But, Daddy," Flossie spoke up, "we *can't* go until Cindy's daddy gets back. We want to meet him."

"Yes," Freddie took up the plea. "And we're going to meet Mr. Evans and tell him all about the man who took his money!"

Mr. Bobbsey laughed. "Well, I can see that you children will be very busy here. Unfortunately, I must get home!"

"Richard," said Mrs. Bobbsey, "why don't you and Dinah go back to Lakeport tomorrow? The twins and I can follow you next week."

When Mr. Bobbsey nodded, she turned to Harry. "Your mother called while you were out and wants us to put you on the train for Meadowbrook tomorrow."

"Oh dear," Dorothy sighed. "Everyone's leaving!"

The following day, Dorothy and Hal drove Harry to the train in the cart while the twins went with Mrs. Bobbsey to see their father and Dinah off. Dinah carried Snoop in his basket, but it had been decided to leave Downy so he could make his home on the pond.

After that, the children were so busy swimming in the ocean and taking boat rides on the lake that the next two days passed very quickly.

Then, early on Monday morning, the telephone rang. Cindy was calling. "Daddy Pete came home yesterday!" she told Nan, who had answered. "We all want you to come to our house this afternoon to meet him."

Uncle William had gone to the city, but Aunt Emily drove Mrs. Bobbsey and the children to the Wellers' small home near the airport. When Cindy ushered them into the living room a tall man with close-cut, brown curly hair rose to greet them.

"So this is the young lady who found my bottle message," he said to Nan with a warm smile. "You'll never know how grateful I am to you!"

"We were all excited about finding a real message," Nan replied, "and especially when we learned it was from Cindy's father!"

"Didn't you get awfully hungry on that island?" Freddie asked.

"Well, Freddie," the captain answered, "I didn't exactly have the best food in the world, but it was enough to keep me alive." He explained that each pilot flying for IAC carried an emergency "survival kit" which contained concentrated foods and first-aid supplies.

"We'd like to hear what happened," Bert said eagerly.

The captain said that his plane had developed engine trouble and had crashed in the ocean. "Before the plane sank," he told them, "I was able to inflate my rubber raft. But unfortunately the radio washed overboard when a particularly big wave hit me. I paddled for a long time and eventually came to a deserted island."

"Is that when you put the bottle in the water?" Nan asked.

Captain Weller nodded. "I had read a good bit about bottle messages," he said. "Since I didn't have any other means of communication, I decided to try that as a last resort. And to think it worked!"

"We're so glad it did, Daddy Pete!" Cindy said happily.

"So am I!" Captain Weller said gravely as he hugged his little daughter. "When I saw that search plane come over last week, I knew that by some miracle my message must have been found!"

At that moment the doorbell rang. Mrs. Weller answered it and returned with a stocky, white-haired man. "Mr. Evans!" the captain cried, rising and shaking the man's hand.

"It was wonderful to learn from the police that you are back, Pete," the newcomer said heartily.

Mr. Evans turned to the Bobbseys and explained that his company had bought many planes from IAC and that he and Captain Weller were old friends.

"I was told I would find you children here. I want to thank you, on behalf of Allied Cargo Airlines, for finding that thief Albert Garry and the money he stole from the plane shipment."

"The twins were happy that they could help," Mrs. Bobbsey spoke up.

"We had fun solving all the mysteries at the seashore," Freddie added.

"Well now, Bobbsey twins," the company president said jovially, "what would you like as a reward?"

There was silence for several seconds. Then

Freddie spoke up. "I'd like another ride in a helicopter!"

When his brother and sisters echoed the little boy's wish, Mr. Evans smiled. "We'll see what we can do," he promised. He left shortly afterwards.

The twins realized that if they were to have another helicopter ride it would have to be soon because they must be home in time for school. When the term did begin, they were to have another exciting adventure, THE MYSTERY AT SCHOOL.

The next morning Mrs. Minturn received a secret telephone call. She asked Dorothy and the Bobbseys to go for a drive with her. After a while she turned into the entrance to the airport.

"Are we really going to have a helicopter ride?" Freddie asked, hardly daring to hope this was true.

"That's only part of the surprise," Aunt Emily said with a smile.

She parked the car and led the way onto the airfield where a large helicopter was waiting. Suddenly the children gasped. From the doorway came Captain and Mrs. Weller and Cindy.

"All aboard for a whirlybird flight to a deserted island!" Captain Weller called, grinning.

"You mean the island where you were rescued?" Bert asked unbelievingly.

"No, that one's too far away. We're going to picnic on another deserted island."

"What fun!" Nan cried.

They all piled in, and soon the helicopter rose into the sky and started up the coast. In about an hour the children could see a small wooded island below them. In the center was a cleared area. Slowly the whirlybird settled down on the grass.

"Our own deserted island!" Flossie cried happily as she ran down the steps of the helicopter.

Captain Weller and his co-pilot carried several large baskets of food from the aircraft. Soon a delicious-looking picnic was spread beneath a large tree, and they all sat down.

"These are awf'ly good 'mergency rations!" Freddie announced as he reached for a third piece of chicken. "I like deserted islands. I don't ever want to be rescued!"

"Not even by sending a message in a bottle?" Dorothy asked teasingly.